ZOE EVANS

CHEER!

CONFESSIONS OF A CHEERLEADER Wannabe

NOV 10 2015

"Bevan vs. Evan
(And other school Rivalries)"

GO ME!

ILLUSTRATED BY BRIGETTE BARRAGER

New York

SIMON SPOTLIGHT

An imprint of Simon & Schuster Children's Publishing Division ★ 1230 Avenue of the Americas, New York, New York 10020 ★ Copyright © 2012 by Simon & Schuster, Inc. All rights reserved, including the right of reproduction in whole or in part in any form. SIMON SPOTLIGHT and colophon are registered trademarks of Simon & Schuster, Inc. Text by Alexis Barad-Cutler

Designed by Giuseppe Castellano

For information about special discounts for bulk purchases, please contact Simon & Schuster Special Sales at 1-866-506-1949 or business@simonandschuster.com.

Manufactured in the United States of America 0212 OFF

First Edition 10 9 8 7 6 5 4 3 2 1

ISBN 978-1-4424-3364-9 (pbk)

ISBN 978-1-4424-3365-6 (eBook)

Library of Congress Control Number 2011933866

You're invited to a

CREEPOVER™

WE DARE YOU . . .

TO CHECK OUT THESE TERRIFIC AND TERRIFYING TALES!

CUPCAKE DIARIES

Middle school can be hard . . .
some days you need a cupcake.

Meet Katie, Mia, Emma, and Alexis—together they're the Cupcake Club. Check out their stories wherever books are sold or at your local library!

CUPCAKE DIARIES
Katie and the cupcake cure
by coco simon

CUPCAKE DIARIES
Mia in the mix
by coco simon

Grace jumped—literally—out of her stare.

"I didn't mean to startle you!" the voice continued. It was Jaci.

"Yeah, sure," said Grace. "So who's that guy over there?" She tried to get her voice back down an octave as she gestured with her chin toward the boy. He had stopped to talk to an older guy with a whistle around his neck.

Jaci snorted. "Oh. *Him. That's* Mike Morris."

water, and snapped them on top of his head. Then he began flinging excess water off his arms. His hair was slicked-back and smooth like a seal's. He looked about her age, or a year older, and was several inches taller, with powerful shoulder muscles. Grace was tall for her age, and usually towered over boys.

She darted a second glance at him, which was time enough to take in the huge green eyes spiked with long eyelashes. He was take-your-breath-away gorgeous. Her paralyzing shyness flooded in like a wave swirling and eddying around rocks.

"You swim too?" he asked. He didn't even look her way, but now bent over to brush the water off his legs.

"Um. Not actually." Not *actually*? Inward groan. "I stink at swimming." *Great. Tell him all your other faults while you're at it*, she thought. *Maybe you can work in what a disaster you are at Spanish*. She prayed her feet wouldn't spontaneously slip out from under her or something.

The boy straightened up and turned to go. "Well, see ya."

"Um, see ya." She turned her body toward Jaci and her chair, but out of the corner of her eye she followed him as he walked away.

"Want to get a snack at the snack bar?" said a voice next to her.

This time she got really high off the board, high enough that she had time to touch her toes, unfold, and stre-e-e-tch her fingers toward the water. *Whoosh!* The bubbles roared in her ears down in the Blue World. She knew it had been a good dive.

As her head emerged from the water, she was startled to see another head not far away from her, near the other springboard. A boy was hanging on to the edge of the pool, wearing tinted goggles, which gave him a froglike look. Where had *he* come from?

"Nice front pike," he called. He had an unexpectedly deep voice, dark brown and velvety.

Grace resisted the urge to dive back down into the Blue World and wait for him to go away. Good thing she was in the cool water, because she felt the usual hot flush rising up to her hairline. "Thanks," she said, and propelled herself to the side of the pool. All she'd done was dive. She had no idea it was called a front spike or whatever he'd said. She pulled herself out of the water and clambered clumsily to her feet, willing herself not to pluck at her wet suit, which was clinging to her in all kinds of embarrassing ways.

The boy swiveled up and out of the pool in one smooth movement, and a moment later was standing a few feet away from her. He pulled up his goggles, drained out the adult,'" said Jaci, putting air quotes around the last two words. "Middle school kids like us have to be here with an adult, but my mom and her friends let us do our own thing. It's great."

"That *is* great," Grace agreed.

"The boys' team is supercompetitive, but they're all annoying jocks, especially their studly star, Mike Morris. They're all about how they look, strutting around in their jammers."

"Jammers?"

"Those tight swim trunks they wear. Speaking of studly—have you checked out Gorgeous Jordan up there? Drool!" She gestured with her chin toward the lifeguard chair at the far end of the other pool, where Jordan Lee, a high school junior, sat surveying the pool like a god looking down from Mount Olympus.

Grace glanced at him. "He's okay." Then she turned back to the water. "I love the diving boards here. I'm going back in. Want to come?"

"Nah, I'm good. I'll be here, studying my irregular verbs." She grinned at Grace.

"Gee, sounds like a laugh a minute," said Grace. She headed back to the diving board.

Step-step-step–drive the knee–JUMP!

"Sure!" Grace said. Did she sound too eager?

"Do you think your parents will let you join RSC for the summer?" asked Jaci. "I mean, it's nice to have you as my guest, but they only let you do that four times a month. It would be cool if you could become a member. I wouldn't mind hanging out with someone with a brain in her head."

"I'm working on it big-time with my mom and dad," said Grace. "I'm doing my chores before they need doing, cranking on my homework before they start nagging, even practicing piano before they ask."

"They'll cave," said Jaci. "Keep up the pressure."

"It *would* be great to join this place." Grace sat down on the edge of her chair and looked around Riverside Swim Club and its huge, T-shaped swimming pool. The diving boards and platforms were just begging to be used. On the other side was another lane pool, filled with splashing kids in one section and serious lane swimmers in the rest. Around the corner was the little-kid pool.

"It's kind of a scene here, though," Jaci continued. "I thought about joining the girls' swim team, but it looks pretty cliquey. Plus I stink at competitive swimming."

"Me too," said Grace.

"The nice thing is, my mom has a zillion friends who belong, and they all take turns being the 'responsible

She swam underwater all the way to the wall. Then she popped to the surface, shook the water from her eyes, and pulled herself out of the pool. She headed over to her chair, where her friend Jaci, wearing huge sunglasses, was reclining and reading a book. Grace glanced down at the book as she grabbed her towel. "You're reading our *Spanish* textbook over Memorial Day *weekend*?"

Jaci shrugged, set down the book, and shimmied up to a sitting position. "We have a vocab quiz tomorrow, remember?"

"Well, I choose to forget, just for a couple of days, how bad I am at Spanish. Every time I ask Ms. Pereira to explain something to me, she answers me in Spanish."

"Yeah, I stink at it, too. That's why I'm brushing up. I really need to improve my grade. Plus I have to get ahead because I have a big clarinet recital coming up."

Grace didn't know Jaci super well, but in the one class they had together (the first class they'd ever had together), she'd quickly realized that Jaci was "That Person"—the kind that walks out of a test moaning about how she's failed it for sure, but then aces it and makes everyone else feel bad about themselves.

"This Thursday I'm allowed to bring a buddy here again," said Jaci. "You want to come with me after school?"

chapter one

Before she could chicken out, Grace took three quick steps forward and jumped.

Her arms flew over her head as she drove her left knee up. She hit the board, then propelled her body up, up, up into the air. As she bent forward, her hips rose above her head and her arms reached for her toes. For a fraction of a second, her body was completely weightless, high above the water at the top of her dive. Then *whoosh*—she unfolded her legs, straightened her body, and reached for the water that was rushing up to meet her. Down she plunged, deep into the sapphire-blue water. Under here it was another place, a Blue World, muffled, safe, her own private domain.

Want more drama?

Here's a sneak peek at a
brand-new series from
Simon Spotlight
coming in May 2012 . . .

Pool Girls

Book 1: Dive In!

I just wanted to see something" moves, which is so LAME. But he didn't. He just kept holding my hand. We walked hand in hand the whole way home, not saying anything. And when I looked at him from the corner of my eye, he was smiling ear to ear.

I guess Cupid finally hit the right guy after all.

GIVE ME A
209!

"You always feel a little guilty," he joked. But it was true. Evan knew me so well.

"Hey, how come you didn't tell me you were trying out?" Evan asked nonchalantly.

"Honestly? Partly because I guess deep down, I thought the fewer people who knew, the less embarrassing it would be if I didn't make it—again. And partly because I knew that telling you would lead to me talking about Katie training me, and I just really didn't want to talk about Katie with you."

"What do you mean? How come?" He tried to look sincere, but he had this smirk on his face that he couldn't hide, and I knew he knew EXACTLY why and he just wanted to hear me say it. BOYS!

"Maybe SuperBoy can help you figure it out," I replied mischievously.

Evan just laughed. Then he told me that Katie said she and Bevan were "talking" again.

"Guess everyone's making up, huh?" I said.

"I don't really care about everyone else," said Evan. "I'm glad we're 'us' again. I've missed you."

And then, the almost impossible/incredible happened. Evan took hold of my hand. And he didn't let it go. I thought he might, like, pretend it was some kind of accident or that he was going to pull one of those "Oh,

GIVE ME A 208!

Ian and Matt shook their heads, but we pulled them in anyway.

When I left practice, Evan was sitting on the floor of the hallway, his sketchbook in hand. I didn't know he was going to wait for me. We'd talked a little bit over the weekend, but it was just our usual kind of talking. Friendly stuff. Neither of us mentioned our moment at the dance, or anything else that's happened recently.

"Hey, what are you working on?" I asked.

"Oh, still this same issue of SuperBoy. I have some changes I'm making to the story. I think Cupid's been shooting the wrong guys."

I smiled.

"Want to walk home together?" he asked sheepishly.

"Yeah."

I told him all about what's been going on with the Titan tryouts, since I hadn't really filled him in on any of it—all the way up to what happened today at practice and how the team reacted when they thought I was leaving them for the Titans.

"I think you did the right thing," said Evan. "There was no point in telling them once you'd already decided to stay with the Grizzlies."

"I still feel a little guilty," I said.

GIVE ME A 207!

to be a Titan. I want to be a Grizzly. But I understand if you're still mad."

"We're not mad," said Tabitha Sue. "We were just surprised."

"Speaking for yourselves," Katarina huffed.

"Hey, wait a minute," said Ian, just noticing something. "Where's Diane?"

Jared pointed across the room to where some Titans had shown up early for their practice. Diane was sitting next to some other newcomers, hanging on to every word Hilary was saying. Jared shook his head in disgust. "She's here, but she's not with us. And to think that I was the one who brought her onto this team!"

"Diane was chosen as an alternate for the Titans, so when I decided not to join, she got my spot," I explained.

"Oh well," said Jared, a little calmer now. "I'll just have to yell at her for keeping secrets from me."

Tabitha Sue came up to me and gave me a hug. "I'm glad you decided to stay. We need you. How else are we gonna rock the Get Up and Cheer! competition coming up?"

Katarina nodded in agreement.

"Awww, you guys. I need you, too!"

"Group hug!" shouted Jared.

GIVE ME A 206!

"I cannot hold this inside a moment longer," he declared. "But I found this outside Coach Whipley's office." He was holding up a piece of paper. My hand flew to my mouth as I realized it wasn't just any piece of paper. It was the results of Titan tryouts. And my name was there for everyone to see! I thought for sure she'd have taken it down by now. But clearly she hadn't.

Jared passed the paper around.

Tabitha Sue looked at it, and then at me. She looked really hurt. "Maddy? Is this true? Are you leaving us?"

She passed it to Katarina. "You trying to be Titan?" she asked angrily.

Then she passed the paper to Matt.

"No—I mean, yes," I said clumsily. "I mean, yes, I did try out, but—"

"Okay, give Maddy a break, you guys," said Jacqui. "She tried out because she needed to do it for herself. You guys know what it's like when you just have to show yourself you can do something, right?"

Everyone nodded.

"But Maddy, why didn't you tell us you were leaving?" said Jared.

"Because I'm not leaving," I said sternly. "You guys, my heart is with you. With the Grizzlies. I don't want

GIVE ME A 205!

Monday, March 14
Evening, dishin' in my kitchen
Song Level:
(Not so) Little Lies

At practice today, everyone was still talking about the dance. Tabitha Sue told everyone that Ricky had asked to join her family at the Pancake House the day before. "He was so adorable with my brother," she gushed. "He helped him cut his pancakes into the shape of a boat. Sooo cute!"

Even Jacqui, who doesn't usually talk about guys with anyone, had ended up flirting with one of Ian and Matt's football friends after our big routine. "Ooh, someone's in loooove!" teased Ian. Matt looked a little beat up about it, but I doubted the love would last very long.

It took me a few minutes to notice that Jared hadn't said anything at all—which was weird, because if anyone had a reason to gloat today, it was him. The dance was his idea, and it was a humongous hit. Finally, he spoke up.

GIVE ME A 204!

the head, and our finale backflips were perfectly timed. GO Grizzlies!

We got a standing ovation from the crowd. "You guys rock!" shouted Katie, as we waved to the audience and ran off to catch our breath.

The rest of the night, all anyone could talk about was the Grizzlies' surprise performance. Evan and I didn't get to dance together again, but no one really split off into couples after that. We all just had a great time. I'm SO happy about the way it all worked out. I'm especially glad that Evan and I are cool now. More than cool, in fact.

Super exhausted. Looking forward to maxin' and relaxin' the rest of this weekend. And for the first time in weeks, I can actually see my floor again! I had forgotten how my design projects can end up taking over my whole room.

GIVE ME A 203!

had slowly realized that the Grizzlies had assembled on the dance floor and were about to knock their socks off.

"Hey!" shouted Clementine into the microphone. "Everyone should be looking at me! I mean, at us!"

Jacqui counted for the team. "Two and a three and a . . ."

She and I led the team through the routine. We danced in perfect synchronization. I could feel everyone hitting their toe touches at exactly the same time. Jared was hamming it up big-time for the crowd, and even Ian and Matt's football buddies started going "Woot! Woot! Woot!" Ian must have loved the attention from his former teammates, because he did a mini break-dance routine.

Jacqui leaned in to my ear. "It's about time they made themselves useful. Remind me to use that in a future routine."

Clementine raced off the stage and was yelling at us to stop. Katie was laughing hysterically, and the whole crowd was clapping to the beat.

The part I was worried about the most, when the girls mock-fall backward and get pulled through the guys' legs, went off without a hitch. Tabitha Sue and Katarina did their cartwheels without kicking anyone in

GIVE ME A 202!

by Katarina and her date, Ethan Tremble, and Jared. The dance turned into just a fun thing and not, like, a gooey romantic thing. Which was totally PERFECT.

Before we knew it, the Dance Committee was announcing the Sunshine Dance king and queen. Absolutely NO ONE was surprised that it was Clementine and her super-jock-y date, Nolan Brown. Clementine got onstage, wiping away tears, as she accepted her crown and bouquet of flowers. She held the bouquet like she was a bride about to throw it to her bridesmaids. Nolan looked like he had other places he'd rather be than onstage with a weepy date.

Clementine was attempting a sort of acceptance speech when Jacqui gestured at me from across the room. It was time. THIS was her perfect moment? Ha-ha!

How can you NOT love Jacqui?!

"Captain?" Jared asked. "Is it showtime?"

"Yup," I replied. "Places, everybody."

"Thank God," said Jared. "This king and queen ceremony is making me vomit in my mouth."

Jacqui cued the DJ. Clementine was still up onstage, waving at the crowd, when the song began. She looked around her like, "Excuse me, I was talking here!," but no one was paying attention to her anymore. The crowd

GIVE ME A 20!!

looked soooo cute.) He definitely had scored his suit from a thrift store, or his dad's closet, but it fit him perfectly. He had even put some hair gel in his hair (but not in a cheesy way).

"Wanna dance?" he asked.

I couldn't believe it. I thought we were fighting, and besides, wouldn't Katie be mad? "But what about—?"

Evan pointed to where Bevan and Katie were dancing (quite cozily). Guess what? I wasn't the tiniest bit jealous ☺.

"Just so you know," said Evan, "I had told Katie I was gonna ask you to dance before she went over to Bevan. So this was my idea."

"I'll make sure to log that in this evening's transcripts," I said to him with a giggle.

We weren't quite sure how to stand at first, but then he placed my hands around his neck and put his hands on my hips. I got a tingly feeling all over. This was real. Evan was dancing with me, and it definitely wasn't just as friends. I didn't want the song to end.

The next song was a Ke$ha song, and everyone in the gym got on the floor. Without even saying anything, we all just ended up dancing as a group, instead of just couples. Me, Jacqui, Lanie, Marc, Ian, Matt, Evan, and Katie. Soon Tabitha Sue and Ricky came over, followed

GIVE ME A 200!

something Katie had said. It was going to be a long night. T.G. Jacqui had come to my rescue.

I went over to where Jacqui was standing. "Hey, thanks for saving me tonight. I was really dreading coming to this thing alone."

"Anytime," she said. "Matt and Ian were all whiny about not having dates, so I told them we'd go with them if they promised to do the routine with us tonight. As you can see, it's a win-win."

"Jacqui, that's awesome! So, when do you think we should do this thing?"

"I'll let you know. I've got the perfect moment in mind."

Not a lot of people were dancing at this point, but by now Mom and Mr. D had arrived and there they were, boogying down. Watching the old people dance gives me the heebie-jeebies. It's like they think every song is a salsa or something. And Mr. Datner is hands down the **WORST** dancer I've ever seen. He tried to do a (bad) imitation of the running man, which made Mom laugh, and I hid my head in shame. Everyone was having a good time. Even the cafeteria ladies who were chaperoning the dance were getting jiggy with it.

Just then I felt a tap on my shoulder. I turned around to see Evan standing there sheepishly. (PS—He

GIVE ME A 199!

work," she directed at Jacqui.

When we all walked into the gym, our jaws dropped to the floor. This didn't look like the place where Grizzly practice happens every day. Or the place where Mr. Datner made us do our stamina and endurance drills. Whoever was in charge of decorating took their job REALLY seriously, because this place looked ridiculously cool! There were a bazillion balloons, papier-mâché suns, big rainbows made of streamers, and even some cotton-candy-esque clouds hanging from the ceiling. In a little corner of the gym with a sign that read, "Moonlight Romance," there was a crescent moon with glittery stars where people could take pics.

I was still wearing my "stunned" face when I spotted Evan walking into the gym arm in arm with Katie. Of course Katie looked bee-utiful. Her dress was a simple red tank number, but it showed off her killer curves and dance/cheer muscles. Her hair cascaded down her back in big waves, and her heels made her look six feet tall. I was sort of wishing she'd break a heel (which I totally felt guilty about five seconds later and then had to "take it back" like a fourth grader).

Evan and I locked eyes, and I gave him a small wave. He smiled briefly at me, then turned his attention to

GIVE ME A 198!

It was hard to find her at first, with all the parents taking pictures and girls clustering together in their little cliques to gossip about what everyone was wearing. Finally, I spotted a girl in a dress that would have made Avril Lavigne proud: It had a black lace top and a huge sash right under the bust, with more black lace below that. And the bottom was an ice gray skirt with pleats. She looked like a gothic fairy-tale princess.

And she looked super relieved to see me. Guess it's possible to feel awkward, even when you're WITH a date at the dance.

"Maaaaads! Aaaaaah!" she yelled as she went in for a hug. (Why do dances make people so sentimental?) "You look uh-mazing."

"I was just about to say the same to you, my friend. Not a safety pin or a skull in sight!"

Lanie did a twirl. "Thank you. I went outside of my comfort zone. But I like it."

I waved hello to Marc, who had definitely snazzed it up in a suit and tie.

"So, good news," I told her, as the rest of my party sauntered up behind me. "Jacqui, Matt, and Ian showed up at my door tonight so I wouldn't have to go to the dance alone!"

"That's awesome!" Lanie said with a smile. "Good

GIVE ME A
197!

I came into the hallway and there, at my doorstep, were Jacqui, Matt, and Ian dressed to the nines. Both Ian and Matt were wearing black suits with bow ties, and Jacqui looked AMAZING in a kelly-green spaghetti strap chiffon dress with a twirly skirt that stopped just above her knees.

"What are you guys doing here?" I exclaimed.

"What, you mean you didn't order two handsome jocks, a rockin' co-captain, and one stunning corsage to go?" Jacqui quipped. "Put it on, and let's go get our groove on."

Of course Mom forced us to take a couple of group pics, but we got to cut it short because Jacqui's mom was waiting for us in the car. I couldn't wait to get out of there—I wanted to be WAY gone before Mr. D arrived. I mean, people would see them at the dance together anyway, but the longer I could keep it off the front page of the Daily Angeles, the better.

Mom sighed, then turned to give me a hug. "Okay, I guess I'll see you there. Have fun!"

"Yeah, uh, you too."

Once we all made it to the parking lot, I started scanning the crowd for Lanie. She and I had agreed she'd walk into the dance with me, and even though I wasn't alone anymore, I didn't want to just ditch her.

GIVE ME A 196!

hair was stick straight and extra luminous. Her makeup was natural-looking and flawless. And her figure was ROCKING in that "conservative" dress we'd both decided on. Oh well, I figured. I'm already going alone to this thing. Who cares if my mom looks as good as a celebrity? Can the night really get worse?

Answer: Oh yes. Yes, it most definitely could. See, when Mom had said picture time, I assumed she wanted me to take pics of her and Mr. Datner. But no, Mom wanted me to pose on our front steps ALL BY MYSELF!

"Mom, I'm, like, the biggest loser at school, going to this dance by myself. Can we please not photograph the evidence?"

Mom brushed a hair out of my eye. "But you look so pretty. You have no idea, Madington. And we can't have this dress of yours go undocumented."

Just then the doorbell rang. I assumed it was Mr. Datner and stepped out of the way so that Mom could open the door. I REALLY didn't want to be there for that moment when he saw her and got all gross and googly-eyed.

But it wasn't Mr. Datner.

"Honey, I think it's for you," Mom said, with a giant grin on her face.

GIVE ME A 195!

Friday, March 11

Post-dance, swooning in my room

Song Level:

Grizzlies Got the Beat

The night of the **BIG DANCE** started out on the less-than-stellar side. I had just finished making myself look positively fantastic. I did my nails in hot pink, used a curling iron in my hair, and cracked open a bunch of makeup that hadn't seen the light of day since my days of playing dress-up (long, long ago). I hoped it wasn't tainted or anything. I could just see myself breaking out in hives in the middle of the dance floor. That would **SO** be my luck. When I was done getting ready, I looked in the mirror. And you know what? I looked **FIERCE**.

And then Mom knocked on my door. "You ready, honey? Picture time!"

"Come in!"

OF COURSE, Mom looked way fiercer than me. She looked like Gwyneth Paltrow at the Oscars. Her

GIVE ME A 194!

I heart that girl so much.

When Diane was finally gone, Mom came running over to me. "Madington, you did it!" she practically screamed. "I saw the list outside Coach Whipley's office. I'm so proud of you, sweetie. How do you feel?"

"I feel great," I told her. And I really meant it. "Getting chosen for the Titans is an amazing feeling. But you want to know what's an even better feeling?"

"What's that, hon?"

"Choosing the Grizzlies over the Titans. I'm not switching teams, Mom. I'm sticking with my team. I'm going to be the best co-captain ever, and we're going to kill it at Get Up and Cheer! this spring."

Mom smiled her thousand-watt smile and pulled me into a mama bear hug. "Madison, I have never been prouder of you than I am right now."

"Let's go home and celebrate."

You know what? Sometimes Mom is all right.

GIVE ME A
193!

"What's going on? I thought you were going to announce your resignation from the team today."

I shook my head. "Nope. Once a Grizzly, always a Grizzly. At least for me."

Her eyes widened in surprise. "Are you serious?"

"I can't help it," I continued. "The Grizzlies are family. But hey, congrats. You're not an alternate anymore."

Diane looked shocked at first, then overjoyed. "Ohmigod! Really?" she squealed.

I noticed Clementine, Hilary, and Katie walking toward their area of the gym for practice. "Yep, really," I said, motioning toward them. "And I think they're just about to find out. You should go talk to them."

"Maddy, I really owe you one." Diane sprinted over to the Titan Triumvirate. The second they saw Diane coming instead of me, Clementine and Hilary shot Katie a look of surprise, and I saw Katie launch into the explanation.

As they walked past me, Clementine gave me the meanest look and coughed "Loser!" under her breath. Well, there goes my brief moment with "nice Clementine." I don't exactly blame her. No one has ever made it to the Titan level and rejected them.

"Oh, grow up, Clem," said Katie.

GIVE ME A 192!

had to prepare for a game. Maybe because performing it at the dance was such a risk. A risk to one's social life, that is.

Mom clapped from her seat on the bleachers. "Nice job, Grizzlies!" She'd shown up a little late today (she was probably off flirting with Ed Phys Ed, tsk, tsk), so I didn't have the chance to tell her that I made the team—or that I decided to turn them down.

"Since you all are so comfortable with this routine, I was thinking we could even kick it up a notch," suggested Jacqui.

I looked over at her, wondering what she had in mind.

"Let's incorporate three toe touches in a row, and some backflips from a standing position."

A couple of people groaned.

"You can do it, guys!" I shouted.

We spent the rest of practice working on the new moves. Everyone was out of breath by the end, so we did an extra-long cooldown.

I noticed that Diane had taken a seat next to me, and wondered how long it would be before she said something. (Answer: not long.) As soon as we were done stretching, and everyone started walking off, she leaned over to me.

GIVE ME A 1911

At practice, I pretended like nothing had happened. I decided that since I'd opted to stick with the Grizzlies, there wasn't really a point in telling them the whole saga. I didn't want to ruin how great everyone's been performing as a team lately—especially on our routine for the dance. I knew Jacqui would be cool when she saw me appear at practice—and I was right.

I walked over to the mat where she was stretching with Tabitha Sue. "Hey, lady," she said with a wink.

"Yo, yo," I said.

When the rest of the team finally trickled in, we had everyone run some laps to warm up. Diane kept jogging up to where I was and throwing me puzzled looks. I think she would have said something, but Tabitha Sue was right behind us. I know she was wondering what I was still doing at Grizzly practice. I figured we could chat after practice.

"All right, we only have a couple more days to nail this routine!" Jacqui announced, when the warm-up was over.

Everyone could practically do the routine in their sleep at this point. It was kind of weird how obsessive we were about getting it perfect—almost like we were more worried about this routine than anything we ever

GIVE ME A
190!

what the outcome was. Though it would have been great to have you on the team."

"Oh, I have a feeling Clementine and Hilary will be more than happy to hear my news."

"Ah, they're not <u>that</u> bad," she said. "They were actually psyched to see how far you've come. You've got skills, like I said."

"Really? Psyched?"

Katie smiled. "Fine, maybe not psyched. But they were impressed. You saw them at tryouts, I know you did. Their faces hardly moved!"

"True, I did notice. It was totally weird."

"Well, don't worry. I'm sure they'll go back to rolling their eyes and giving you the stink eye once I tell them you're turning us down," she replied with a wink.

OMG she's totally right. I'm doomed. DOUBLE UGH.

I watched her ponytail swing back and forth as she sashayed out of the classroom. I thought about how back in the day I would have killed to walk arm in arm with the Triumvirate, our ponytails swinging in synchronized motion. But that was then, and this is now. Looks like I'm not going to be a Titan after all, and I'm more than OKAY with it. In fact, I'm thrilled to be a Grizzly. ROAR!

GIVE ME A
189!

"I don't know how to say this, Katie. I'm so grateful for everything you did for me. I mean, you are amazing. I'm so honored to have made the cut for the Titans, but . . . I just am not ready to leave the Grizzlies. I'm really sorry," I said, covering my face in shame.

Katie reached out to peel my fingers away from my eyes. "Whoa, hey. Calm down, Mads. It's okay."

I looked at her hopefully. "It is? You're not mad?"

Katie shook her head. "Not at all. Listen, I know a thing or two about feeling torn. Remember how I didn't know if I was ready to leave the Titans for dance school?"

I nodded.

"See? It's the same. Except in your case, the choice was yours to make. It didn't work out that way for me. I heard back from the school in New York, and I didn't get in."

"Oh, I'm so sorry, Katie."

"It's cool. The truth is, I don't think I would have gone, after all. I still love where I'm at. Just like you do."

I felt a huge wave of relief wash over me. For the first time in days, my shoulders released from their Hunchback of Notre Dame position.

"It was fun training you," said Katie. "I don't care

GIVE ME A
188!

but Lanie put her hand on my arm.

"Okay. Are you absolutely positive that you want to be a Grizzly permanently?"

I smiled. "Yeah. It's _my_ team. I don't want to walk away from everything we've done together."

I texted Katie to meet me in "our" classroom after lunch. When she came into the room, she ran right up to me to give me another hug. Hello, spontaneous bursts of affection!

She was already wearing her Titan uniform— which I think they always do on days when they get new recruits, and sometimes the day before really important competitions—to boost team spirit and all. I took a good look at it, reminding myself that what I was about to say to Katie would mean that the only time I'll ever get to wear it is when I play dress-up in Mom's uniform. (Which, PS, doesn't fit me because Mom is shaped like a model and me? Not so much. Oh, and, which, PPS, I totally don't do anymore because I'm not four.)

"Hey, what's the matter? You look like you ate the mystery meat loaf at lunch," said Katie, registering the look on my face. (I'm so bad at hiding my emotions.)

"You're gonna kill me," I said.

"No, I won't. What's going on?"

GIVE ME A 187!

"Okay, Miss Hays. Will you repeat that one more time for the record? I want to make sure I have this down right."

I swiped at her pen. "Hey, I'm being serious."

"Sorry. I just had a feeling this would happen."

"So, you think that's the right thing to do? To stay with the Grizzlies?" I really needed to hear a clearheaded piece of advice, and Lanes ALWAYS gives it to me straight (or "street," as Katarina would say, hee-hee).

"I don't know if it's what's <u>right</u>, but it's what <u>you want. Isn't it?"</u>

"Yeah, it is. But I don't know how to tell Katie. I feel like she'll be so disappointed."

Lanie gave me her "what I'm about to say is serious" face. "Look, I'm not the biggest fan of Suzie Cheerleader myself. But I have a feeling that she's not going to sweat it as much as you think. She helped train you because she thought it was what you wanted."

I thought about how I hadn't wanted to tell Jacqui about tryouts for the same reason. And that turned out okay.

"All right," I said. "I'll tell her after lunch. I need to get this over with." I went to gather my things,

GIVE ME A
186!

team just so I could prove to myself that I'm worthy of the Titans? That they aren't better than me?

"You okay?" asked Katie.

I plastered on a megawatt smile. "Oh yeah! I was just wondering where my mom is. I want to go tell her the news!" I hate lying, but I had to cover for my sudden change in mood.

Katie smiled back at me. "We did it, Mads!"

I gave her a high five. "Couldn't have done it without you."

The whole rest of the day I agonized over my decision. If I was going to back out of the Titans, I'd have to do it today, before practice. And if I was going to stick with them, I'd need to find a way to tell the Grizzlies I wasn't coming back. Talk about awkward. I met up with Lanes in the afternoon to discuss.

"Mads, you look like you're having heart palpitations. I thought the nervous thing would end now that you found out you made the team."

I sighed deeply. "I know! Sometimes I wonder if I create problems for myself. Anyway, here's the thing. Now that I made the team, I'm not so sure I want in anymore."

Lanie grabbed the notebook where she wrote down all her notes and ideas for the Daily Angeles.

GIVE ME A 185!

I felt a tap on my shoulder. It was Katie, who looked like she was going to burst with happiness. "You did it!" she squealed.

"Omigod! I can't believe it!" I said to her, as we hugged.

"Yep. Seriously. I'm so happy for you, Mads!"

We jumped up and down for a few moments, whooping with joy. But I realized that underneath my initial excitement, I was feeling something really strange. It was that doubt again. This time the doubt didn't have to do with me not making the Titans. This time I was doubting whether or not I actually wanted to BE a Titan, now that I have the chance.

"Stop it, heartstrings!" I reprimanded myself. "Stop being such a Goody Two-Shoes. You wanted this just as badly as brain did."

All I heard back was, "But what about your team, Madison?" (In this super-annoying pip-squeaky voice.)

SO uncool.

This was what I always wanted. Right? The thing I'd dreamed about since the moment I first held a pom-pom. And now I was willing to let it go for a second-rate team? Why? And why did I go to all this trouble to try out if I wasn't even going to accept the bid? That's when it hit me: Had I tried to make the

GIVE ME A 184!

this gesture?). Then I turned around and ran toward the phys ed offices.

When I got there, a huge crowd had already formed around the piece of paper that was taped to the wall. But before I could start shoving my way through the crowd, I noticed a very depressed-looking Diane slumped on the floor. She was like a poster child of rejection.

Since I have this thing called a heart, I squatted down to talk to her. I didn't even have to ask.

"I didn't make it," she volunteered. Her eyes looked like she'd been crying.

"You're kidding!" I exclaimed.

She looked away from me, to a piece of lint on the floor. "Well, technically I didn't make it, but I guess the 'good news' is that I'm an alternate. But you did." She pointed to the paper on the wall.

"What? I <u>did</u>?" I wanted to grab her into a hug, but figured this wasn't the best moment for sharing joy.

She nodded solemnly. "Yep. Go see."

As I made my way through the crowd toward the list, random girls patted me on the back. "Congrats, Madison!" said one. "Nice job!" said another.

And there I was. Right after Simone Jacobs.

I can't believe it. I AM A TITAN!!!!

GIVE ME A 183!

Mr. Cooper cleared his throat uncomfortably. "Very well."

FREEDOM!

I booked it down the hallway, nearly shoving a girl out of my way as I rounded a corner. Then I almost ran over Bevan—the last person I was thinking about that morning.

Bevan grabbed me by both shoulders before I smacked right into him. "Whoa, cowgirl! Where's the rodeo?"

"Sorry," I said, trying to catch my breath. "The list was just posted from tryouts, and I'm dying to see it."

Bevan raised an eyebrow. "Tryouts? For the Titans?"

I nodded. "Yeah."

"I didn't know you were trying out!"

"Well, no one did, really. It was a secret."

Bevan looked at me like he was proud. Weird. "Good for you. I had no idea."

We stood there smiling at each other. It was nice to be talking like friends.

"So what are you waiting for?" he said, playfully shoving me away. "Go, go, go!"

I started jogging backward. "All right, all right! Talk to you later!"

He gave me a dorky salute (what is it with guys and

GIVE ME A 182!

The thing that really SUCKED was that the results wouldn't be posted until after first period. How would I survive through class?

It was like my prayers had been answered (hallelujah!) when Mr. Cooper decided to show a DVD of Romeo and Juliet—a really old version (not the one with Leonardo DiCaprio ☹)—during English.

"You kids need to appreciate fine filmmaking," said Mr. Cooper. He cleared his throat. "In addition, of course, to appreciating Shakespeare."

At his announcement, the whole class let out a big round of applause. But I don't think they were appreciating filmmaking OR Shakespeare. More like having a class to doze off, zone out, or pass notes during. Poor Mr. Cooper. But at least it seemed that perhaps the cheer gods were smiling down on me after all.

I actually stayed awake through the whole class. I don't think my nerves would have let me fall asleep. I was staring at my watch like it contained the secrets of life. When it finally hit the hour, I sprinted up from my seat even before the bell rang.

"Miss Hays, do you have an appointment we should all know about?"

A few people snickered.

I blushed. "Sorry. Um, just really need the ladies' room."

GIVE ME A 18!!

starting to seem like we really weren't talking anymore. I can't even really remember at this point who hurt who. He asked me to the dance, but I already had a date. He was upset because I hadn't mentioned anything about having a date. Five seconds later, I got rid of said date, but oops! Too late. After pining for all of a nanosecond, Evan got past everything and asked someone else. Of course, when he was upset, I was trying to reach out and apologize. But now that I'm the one who's upset, he's nowhere to be found. Ugh. BOYS!

The one thing that DID calm me a little bit was finishing up my dress. Late last night I fixed the hemline and worked on making the pleats as perfect as possible. It was basically done—it just needed a few sequins sewn on here and there.

This morning I zoomed through breakfast, practically throwing Cheerios down my throat and chasing them with a few glugs from the milk carton (Mom wasn't looking, so I was safe). Today was the day. FINALLY I was going to find out if I'd made the squad or not. On the car ride to school, I didn't even want the radio on.

"I just need to think," I told Mom.

"Silence is good for the soul," she said approvingly. Yeah. Okay, Buddha.

GIVE ME A 180!

Monday, March 7

Song Level:

Runaway Titan

Rah!
Rah

Yeah. What I said before about not freaking out?
Whatevs. This weekend was FREAKOUT-O-RAMA. I
couldn't sit still for a second, my nerves were buzzing
so much. Mom even asked me to do some yoga with her,
"to center my chi." Um. Yeah. Only if I can do the new
"Oh No She Didn't" pose the whole time.

Lanes came over to watch a movie on Sunday, but
she could tell my heart wasn't in it.

"Why don't you just call Katie?" she urged. "She
would tell you if you made it or not."

I threw a cheeto at her. "Are you kidding? She's a
captain. Katie knows the rules. Besides, I don't want to
take advantage of our friendship."

"Suit yourself, Nervous Nelly," said Lanie.

"Very funny," I said.

I still hadn't heard from Evan, either. It was

GIVE ME A
179!

don't like me? And on top of that list: Am I really and truly ready to leave my Grizzly buds in the dust? I can worry all I want, but it doesn't really matter until I know the results on Monday. It's time to somersault toward a bubble bath and soak these achy muscles.

One more thing: I wish I could call Evan and tell him how today went. If we weren't in this stupid "fight" (is that what it is?), I wouldn't think twice. But then I'd have to explain that Katie had helped me with training, and that would bring up a subject I really wasn't in the mood to talk about: Katie and Evan. Or the fact that now I'm going solo to the biggest school event of the year.

Well, I guess what "they" say is true. You REALLY can't have it all.

Big sigh.

GIVE ME A
178!

you. Even though I'll really miss having you on the team."

I laughed. "Well, we'll just have to see what happens before we start saying our good-byes."

I'll have to remind myself in the future that when in doubt, I SHOULDN'T doubt. People are awesome. Especially cheerleaders. Yaaaaay, Jacqui!

This time, walking back to my mom's car wasn't a walk of shame. I nearly did a couple of flips toward the car.

I feel really good about how I did today. Even if I didn't make it, I know I gave it my all.

Mom looked a little worried until she saw the smile on my face. "So?" she asked.

"Well, I won't know till Monday. But I have a good feeling." I threw my bag into the backseat.

"Get in, you little superstar, you. This occasion calls for ice cream."

I rolled my eyes. "Mom, I'm not five."

Mom looked a little disappointed.

"Uh, who cares? Everyone loves ice cream!"

As I went to town on my raspberry ice-cream cone, I tried not to let any doubt ruin my warm and fuzzy feelings. Doubts like, what if Diane gets my spot (even though I kicked her butt on mat)? Or what if Clementine and Hilary reject me just because they

GIVE ME A 177!

this time I've got to get through two whole days of being in the dark! I don't know if I can take it. Grrr. Katie beamed at me as I walked out of the gym, but I knew she couldn't give anything away. She was proud of me, though. Even Clementine gave me a head nod.

It was time to face Jacqui. She was sitting on the bottom bleacher, saying "good job" and "nice out there" to the people she knew.

"So," she said. "How long have you been planning to try out?" She didn't say it in an accusing way. I could tell she just wanted to know.

"It was on my mind for a while," I admitted. I felt so horrible. "But I didn't decide for real until, like, a week ago." I played with a tiny string that was hanging from my tank top. "I just didn't know how to tell you."

"Madison," said Jacqui. "You shouldn't keep something like this from your co-captain. You know I would have supported you no matter what." Her dark curls waved back and forth as she shook her head emphatically.

"I didn't want you to bug out at me. I don't know . . . My head has been so weird lately. I feel like everything I do is wrong."

"Oh, come on," said Jacqui, nudging me playfully in the arm. "Seriously, you're awesome, girl. Don't let anyone tell you otherwise. I'm crossing my fingers for

GIVE ME A
176!

I wanted to hit myself on the head for not having told her. Jacqui's my friend, my co-captain. How could I have left her in the dark?

I took my position on the mat, but I couldn't get the image of Jacqui's hurt face out of my head.

I closed my eyes. I had to zone everything out. Diane's skills, Diane's wipeout, Jacqui's face, the Grizzlies. "Concentrate," I told myself. "Look excited and confident. Get in the zone."

I took four strides, and then my legs were up in the air, doing a high front hurdler. Then I did a back round-off to back handspring into a full. With NO MISTAKES! Woot woot! Katie was smiling ear to ear, and even Clementine and Hilary looked impressed. Which basically just meant that they kept their faces completely still instead of snickering or rolling their eyes at me. I have to admit, it was a little hard to get used to.

Most of the other girls did basic cartwheels and round-offs. A few did back handsprings, but no one else did anything half as advanced as me and Diane.

When tryouts were over, I felt like I'd never be able to walk again. My legs were absolute jelly. Coach Whipley announced that we'd find out the results on Monday!! So annoying. Last time we found out right away, and

GIVE ME A
175!

I could even tell that Clementine and Hilary were impressed. They were smiling at Diane as she flipped in the air. That is, until her landing. She must have overshot it, because next thing we all knew, Diane was tripping over her knees and falling face-first onto the floor. She looked like a Gumby with no motor control.

Props to Diane, she didn't let it show on her face. She kept smiling and looking confident.

Loud "oohs" echoed throughout the gym. Talk about embarrassing! I had to admit, I felt horrible for her (even though she was the competition). Up until this moment, Diane and I had been nearly neck and neck in terms of tryouts. If I messed this up, we would be in the same boat. If I aced it, I'd be leaving her behind in the dust.

Before I knew it, it was about to be my turn at the mat. I happened to look over at the bleachers, and what I saw nearly stopped my heart from beating. It was Jacqui! I had no idea what she was doing there at first. But then I realized it made sense. This was her first time not at Titan tryouts, so she probably just wanted to see how everything went down. But this was BAD. She didn't look too happy. Not angry, but I don't know . . . maybe disappointed? She saw me looking at her and gave me a quick thumbs-up. I felt sooooo guilty.

GIVE ME A
174!

us the cheer. There were a lot of arm motions and just one jump, but again, it wasn't **THAT** bad. I realized then that tryouts weren't so much about challenging cheerleaders to perform the world's toughest moves or cheers—it was seeing how people performed under pressure. That's what killed me last time. I freaked.

Spazzmadstic Madison kept herself hidden away for most of the morning. We had to perform the dance routine as a group, and I stayed completely focused. I even did a good job of not looking at Diane so I wouldn't get spooked. (Maddy, 1; Spazzmadstic Madison, 0. Woohoo!) There **WAS** a split second where I almost went left when we were supposed to go right, but I corrected myself before anyone could see (or at least I hoped).

When it was time for tumbling, I noticed that most people who were trying out really aren't at my level **AT ALL**. They were more like me last year, minus any coordination. There were a few pretty good cheerleaders, but not really anyone who I was worried would take my slot. So there I was, tooting my own horn, when Diane suddenly catapulted herself across the map in a string of three beautiful back handsprings into a really high back tuck. And she wasn't just good, she was **REALLY** good. Suddenly, the competition was **ON**. For realz.

GIVE ME A 173!

the Titans in front of us. Luckily, Katie had taught me a way to remember a longer routine: You attach a letter of the alphabet to each move. "Arms up" is A. "Hip thrust" is H. And so on. Then you just remember the letters, and hopefully you remember the routine. In the best-case scenario, the letters almost spell a very not grammatically correct sentence.

"All right, five-minute break," shouted Hilary. "We're doing cheers next."

I went over to my gym bag to grab a water. I was doing okay so far. Maybe this wasn't going to be as bad as I feared? But before my mind wandered over into Blissful Titanhood Land, I talked some sense into myself. Last year I had made the mistake of getting carried away with the thought that I'd make the team, and when I didn't make it I was completely destroyed. This time I tried to tell myself to live in the now. Don't think about making it or not making it. Just get through this, and do your best trying.

Diane was gulping down her water like she'd been crawling for miles through a hot desert. I know it was mean, but I couldn't help but think, "Not so smart. Unless you like a side of stomach cramps with your tryout meal."

We reported back to the mats so Hilary could teach

GIVE ME A 172!

I nodded. "Yeah, I hear you. I guess I'm just surprised to see you."

"Likewise," she said with the slightest smirk. "What are you doing here?"

"I want to challenge myself too," I said with a smile. But underneath I was thinking, "This girl better not take my slot!"

The Titans lined up at the front of the mat to show us the drill. First, they played the music so we'd get a sense of the rhythm. It was a high-speed version of Katy Perry's "Firework." The routine wasn't too hard. It seemed like they were looking to see how quickly we could learn something new, and how tight we could get a routine in a short period of time.

"Straight arms, quick, sharp motions," I repeated to myself. It was hard to forget the last tryouts—when I was totally tripped up by Jared because of his flailing jazz hands. (T.G. we've gotten those under control!) But this time, it wasn't Jared I had to worry about. It was Diane. And the fact that I was standing right behind her made this feel like a too-easy game of Simon Says. Everything she did, I did. We looked like twins!

"Okay, ignore everyone else," I said to myself. I did my best to take everything in so I'd remember it later, when we would have to perform it without

GIVE ME A
171!

took a seat. I like the middle of the mat because it gives me the best view of the Titans up front who are leading us through the routine. I started stretching my arms out, when I noticed a familiar profile in front of me: DIANE!!!

What was SHE doing there? All that time and energy voting her onto the Grizzlies and getting her up to speed on our routines, and she secretly was training to be a Titan? I was so angry I could have screamed. But then I remembered I was guilty of the same thing, in a way. The real reason I was angry? Diane is GOOD. And the fewer good people trying out, the better for me. Boo.

"Hey, Diane," I said from behind.

Diane literally jumped, then she turned around. "Oh, wow. Maddy, I didn't expect you to be here."

"You either." I guess we were both caught red-handed. Or pom-pom-handed. "Diane, I thought you hated those girls." I motioned toward Clementine and Hilary, who were reviewing the routine among themselves.

"Well, I'm not, like, their biggest fan," she whispered. "But being a Grizzly helped me realize I'm pretty good at cheer. I want to challenge myself, you know? And I figure I can swallow my pride if it means cheering with a team like the Titans."

GIVE ME A 170!

down at some papers. Probably the list of kids trying out. Clementine was staring right at me, with a puzzled look. Then I think I detected (gasp!) the slightest smile. Could it be that Katie was right? Does Clementine Prescott have a . . . heart?

As I walked farther into the gym, I recognized some of the people who had tried out last year and didn't make it, but decided NOT to join the Grizzlies. Rebecca Simmons had been pretty good, but she froze when it was her turn to show the judges her cheers. She'd been so upset about not making it that she didn't show up to school for almost a week. Her mom had called in saying it was "exhaustion," but we all knew the truth. Today she looked ready to out-cheer Coach Whipley.

Almost.

Coach Whipley was frantically barking orders at everyone. It is always like this at tryouts. People are so buzzed and excited they can hardly stand still, and everyone wants to get one last move in before tryouts begin. "Everyone, on the mat!" she shouted. "No more gossiping! No more tumbling! If you're not sitting still on the mat in thirty seconds, you'll be leaving this gym!"

That got everyone in order. Any stragglers quickly left their little cliques, wished each other luck, and

GIVE ME A 169!

there. I threw it in there anyway. You can never have too many snacks.

When we were in the car, I asked her the question I'd been avoiding. "Mom, you're really okay with this? You're being so cool about me trying out for the other squad."

Mom gazed out the window wistfully. "For me, it's bittersweet. You know I always want the best for you. And the Titans really are of a different caliber. So of course I want you to go for it. But at the same time, I'll miss getting to coach you every day, and I'll miss watching you grow into an amazing captain."

I was glad Mom was being honest.

"I'll miss having you as my coach too. But I'll still need your help on, well, anything involving cheer."

Mom gave me a wink. "I hope so."

The first person I saw when I walked into the gym was Katie. She ran up to me and gave me a hug, without saying anything. I felt something scratchy in my neck. It was a note (Katie's fave form of communication). It was folded into a tiny square, with a smiley face sticker holding it closed.

I unwrapped the note. "Remember, be confident. You've so got this. Rock it out today!"

I looked back at her to smile, but she was looking

GIVE ME A 168!

The truth was, I could barely breathe from all my nerves, let alone swallow lumpy oatmeal. I began to wonder who else would show up today. Would I be competing against random hidden talents? Or would there be more Jared and Tabitha Sue types (the pre-Grizzly versions of them)? Would someone who I'd never thought had a cheer background just pop up out of nowhere and wow the judges? And of course, my **WORST** fear: that someone from the Grizzlies would show up. It was a Saturday, after all, but you never know. What if Matt or Ian left a towel or jock strap (or whatever it is those guys wear)? **OR** what if someone from the Grizzlies **ACTUALLY** tried out??

With each bite, I reviewed another move that Katie and I had practiced together. Chew, toe touch. Chew, pike jump. Chew, herkie.

"I hope I can keep this down. I'm even more nervous than last time," I told Mom.

Mom came up behind me and put her hand on my shoulder. "Nerves mean that you're about to do something great," she said, whispering into my ear.

She always says that.

I grabbed a PowerBar to toss into my bag for later, but soon realized that Mom had already put one in

GIVE ME A
167!

stop myself from trying to cheer along with every Titan video I watched, but when the clock hit eleven, I knew it was time to get my snooze on.

Mom bounced out the door, reminding me to make time for breakfast. "Yeah, yeah," I said wearily.

I found a neatly folded pile of cheer tryout clothes waiting for me on top of my dresser. Mom had thought of everything, as usual: sweatpants, cheer shorts, two T-shirts, two sports bras, and a hoodie.

Getting dressed is a cinch when someone else does all the work! I quickly brushed my hair, put on some light makeup, kissed my pom-pom for good luck, and went downstairs.

"Mmmm. Hard-boiled egg and bland oatmeal. Delish," I said as I surveyed this morning's lame-o menu.

"You don't want to eat a bunch of sugar before tryouts," said Mom. "You'll crash."

I know she's absolutely right, but I like giving her a hard time sometimes. Especially when she's in "cheer mom" mode. And this morning it was in full overdrive.

"Mom, don't you know Pop-Tarts are the breakfast of champions?"

Mom rolled her eyes at me. "Maybe video game champions."

"Ha."

GIVE ME A
166!

Saturday, March 5

Late afternoon, on my front steps

Song Level:

Let's Bring It On

Woke up this morning with a serious case of déjà vu. Mom tickled me under my nose with my ratty old pom-pom to wake me up, just like she did at last tryouts (or any big day of mine, for that matter).

"Sleepy Maddy, wakey-wakey!" she sing-songed.

I wiped the sleep from my eyes. "Ughhhh. Too bright!" Mom had opened all the shades, and the sun was blasting down on me.

"Oh, no. You've got your big day today. Drink in the sunshine! Up and at 'em!"

Mom lifted both arms to the sky as if lifting the sun itself. Of course she was up and dressed hours ago. Her gardenia perfume left little trails behind her as she moved about my room.

I sat up in bed and stretched my neck, which was killer sore from my late night workout. I almost couldn't

GIVE ME A 165!

spots from here on out. Tonight I'm going to review all the top Titan videos and make sure there isn't anything I've missed. Judges, watch out. Madison Hays is coming to a mat near you!

    J-J-J-Jitters!

Mom sat on the bed and put each one back on the hanger.

"When can you show me your final dress?" she said, smoothing out the crinkles in the chosen one.

"The night of. It's a surprise."

"So exciting!"

I showed Mom some of the cheers I've been practicing for tryouts. (This Saturday!! Eeek!) I'm glad I finally told Mom that I'm planning on trying out, because (a) I can practice at home without worrying about her asking why, and (b) she can help me with anything I'm not getting. Mom said the only thing I need to work on is my "cheer face."

"Always smile, always look the judges in the eye, and look psyched to be there."

"That's exactly what Katie told me," I said. "What, are you and Katie, like, sharing brain waves or something?"

Mom shrugged. "Well, we're both Titans. I remember that was one of the major things we looked for in new members. The Titans are known for looking like they're having a better time than anyone else. But it takes effort."

I can't believe tryouts are just a few days away. Katie and I are going to concentrate solely on my weak

GIVE ME A 163!

When we got home, Mom wanted to show me the different dresses she was thinking of wearing to the dance. "You're the fashionable one, Maddy. I need your advice."

We went up to her room, and she hummed while she went into her closet to get the dresses. I noticed that there was an unframed photo of Mom and Mr. Datner on top of her dresser and decided not to comment on it.

"So," said Mom, "which one do you like better?"

She pointed to an emerald-green strapless that went to the knee and would definitely bring out her eyes. But it was a little too much, in my opinion, for the school dance. I shook my head.

"Okay, what about this?" She held up a navy tank dress that had kind of an Audrey Hepburn feel to it.

"Ooh, that one! And you should do a chignon."

Mom clapped. "Oh, good! I was hoping you'd say this one."

"You could even do, like, red lipstick."

Mom smiled. "Great idea. Just to make sure—you're not into this one, right?" She picked up Dress Numero Tres, which was a one-shouldered long dress. It was pretty, but again, didn't feel school-dance-chaperone-ish.

"I still like what's behind door number two better."

GIVE ME A
162!

"Zis ees rediculousness. I am queen of round-off!" said Katarina, stomping back to position.

"Want some help?" offered Diane.

Katarina shook her head. "I must do zis all alone." She went for it again, and landed gracefully.

After a few more rounds of rehearsing everyone's weak spots, we got together for the last run-through of the day.

"You guys were awesome!" I told everyone, when we were finished. We high-fived all around.

"The last part is so cool," said Jacqui. "Go Grizzlies!"

Everyone left practice in good spirits.

"You wanna work on some of our own stuff?" asked Jacqui. We hadn't done that in a while—since I'd usually have spent all my energy practicing earlier in the day with Katie. Which of course, Jacqui didn't know about. I couldn't say no, though, or it would seem weird. Also, I've missed all our post-practice workouts lately.

"Yeah," I said cheerfully. I was still a little rough around the edges with my back handspring, so I suggested we practice that for a while.

Jacqui's, of course, were flawless. She's so good at tumbling. Jacqui gave me some pointers on my back handspring, and I practiced until I got dizzy. Funny, I kind of have two Titans training me for tryouts.

GIVE ME A
16!!

"Ha, okay, Mrs. soccer star."

"Make that ex-Mrs. soccer star."

Jacqui's eyes almost popped out of her head in shock. "What do you mean? What happened?" she asked, all concerned.

"It's okay. We're just not right for each other. He's been way too busy with soccer, and it just didn't seem right to go to the dance together, so I told him we shouldn't."

"Oh, Maddy, I'm sorry!" she exclaimed, and put her arm around me in a half hug. "That really stinks."

"Yeah, kinda. But it's okay. Hey, now we don't have to go to the dance alone—we can go together."

"Still kinda lame, but I'll take it," she joked.

When we stopped chatting, we looked over at Matt and Ian, who were really killing the dance routine. "They're doing a pretty good job, huh?" I said to her.

"Yeah, they're actually not such bad dancers," Jacqui replied, seeming suddenly deep in thought. "Maybe they're finally going to be of some use to us."

Tabitha Sue asked if we could review the part where she and Katarina would do left-handed cartwheels into round-offs.

"Nice!" I shouted, as Tabitha Sue nailed it. Katarina had a little too much momentum and wobbled at the end.

GIVE ME A 160!

doesn't feel so great. Now that I think about it, I'm kind of avoiding two people. It wouldn't be fun to run into Bevan, either. Then again, what are the chances? I never see him these days, and based on past experience, even if I did, he probably wouldn't notice me. Luckily, it's an unusually warm day for March. Otherwise I'd be turning into an icicle right about now.

At least being alone means I have time to write.

THAT NIGHT, LIVE FROM MY LIVING ROOM!

Practice tonight lifted my saggy spirits. We rehearsed and rehearsed our routine, and by the end of practice we were REALLY good! Even Ian and Matt were getting into it, correcting each other when they each messed up.

"Check it. Your arm goes <u>this</u> way, not <u>that</u> way," Ian instructed Matt.

Matt put his hands on his hips, furrowing his brow in concentration. "Wait, show me again?"

"Why don't you two go to the mats over there and practice that part?" suggested Jacqui.

"You wanna join?" Matt asked Jacqui with a wink.

I couldn't help but laugh. "I don't know," I whispered to Jacqui. "I think you two would make a pretty cute couple."

GIVE ME A 159!

jeans with the safety pins in them."

"Well, I was planning on wearing my Save Metal T-shirt over a tank dress. . . ."

"Oh please no," I pleaded.

"Just kidding!"

I dramatically let out a breath of relief.

"Gee. Ye of little faith. I'm wearing a cute dress I ordered from the Delia's catalog. You'll approve, I promise."

I raised my eyebrow at her skeptically. "A dress? You must really like this guy."

After my convo with Lanes, I made a resolution: I'm not going to think about Evan or the dance, or Katie (except when it came to cheer stuff) for the rest of the day. My brain needs a rest from that kind of drama. I decided to only focus on training for tryouts, and leave this mess behind. I told Lanes that I was gonna grab lunch to go so I don't have to sit with Evan at lunch and feel even worse. She tried to convince me to come to the caf, and said she would just talk about herself all through lunch so neither of us would feel awkward. But I said no thanks. UNFORCH, eating lunch on the steps at school alone is not the sweetest of experiences. I don't mind being alone in general, but when the reason is because I'm avoiding someone, it

GIVE ME A 158!

going to the dance with Mr. Datner, that I wasn't going to the dance with Bevan anymore, and that I'd tried to ask Evan to the dance but he was already going with Katie.

Lanie laughed so hard she almost squirted chocolate out of her nose.

"What are you, like, five?" I asked her.

"Sorry, sorry," said Lanie, wiping her face. "I just think it's kind of hilarious. Your mom has a date to the dance and you don't!"

"Wow. Thanks, Lanes. Good thing I went to you to feel better."

"I'm sorry," she said, stifling one last laugh. "It really sucks. You're still gonna go to the dance, right?"

I nodded. "I sort of refuse to not show my masterpiece to the world," I said, thinking about my dress. "So yeah, I'm going."

"You're gonna look so fab, Bevan and Evan are both going to wish they were there with you," said Lanie.

"Thanks. Promise you'll include me on the dance floor so I don't look like a complete loser?"

"Cross my heart!"

"While we're on the subject," I said, "we need to discuss what you're wearing. Are you still going with the pantsuit? And if not, please say it's not those black

GIVE ME A 157!

Last night, I could so picture Evan with ME at the dance. So how can he be going with someone else?

And now, this means I'll DEFINITELY have a seat reserved for me at the dance next to Abby Lincoln.

I texted Lanes before class started. "The Lounge. Emergenceee. After class."

"On it," she wrote back immediately.

In class Mr. Cooper was talking about the great tragic loves in literature and asking us to name a few. I couldn't stop thinking of Evan and me. I could see what the cover of our story would look like.

Luckily, he didn't call on me all through class, or I probably would have blurted out, "She can't go with him! Neveerrrrrr!"

I felt guilty, though. I didn't want Katie to go to the dance alone, either. But I know if Evan hadn't asked her, someone else would have.

I couldn't WAIT for class to be over. I was dying to talk to Lanes. I practically sprinted to the Lounge, nearly running over a very small girl who was two classes below me. "Oops! Sorry! In a rush!" I shouted behind me.

Lanie was already waiting for me, sipping chocolate milk. "What's the emergency?"

I told her almost all in one breath that Mom was

GIVE ME A 156!

Just then Katie walked by. She was in a super-happy mood. "Hey, guys! We're all going to have so much fun at the dance! I'm so excited!" she said, putting an arm around each of us. "Gotta run, talk to you both later!"

"We?" I asked him.

Evan nodded. He looked a little sorry.

I felt like one of those punching bags that Mr. Datner made us drag across the floor.

"So, um, what happened with you and Bevan?"

I was so NOT in the mood at that moment to tell him what happened. I shrugged, trying not to look as horrible as I felt. "It just . . . didn't feel right."

"Look," said Evan, biting his lower lip, "I'm sorry, but I gotta go."

"Later."

I couldn't believe Evan and Katie were going together. When I'd told Katie that tons of guys must have been building up the courage to ask her to the dance, I never thought that Evan, MY Evan, was one of them. I know that Evan and Katie are just friends, but I can't help but be jealous. What if Katie shows up at the dance looking more amazing than ever, and the two of them have the BEST time, and next thing I know, they're a couple? That would be totally Twilight Zone-y. The two of them together doesn't make sense to me.

GIVE ME A 155!

When he saw me, he smiled a little, then put his head down as if to ignore me.

I walked up to meet him halfway. "Hey," I said.

"Hey."

"Can you talk for a minute?"

Evan looked toward the door to his classroom. "I have to get to class."

"Evan, you have, like, fifteen minutes before first bell."

"All right," he said. He buried his hands deep in his pockets and leaned against a nearby locker.

There was no way to do this other than just get it out there. Like I did with Bevan.

"I want to go with you to the dance," I said. And as soon as I said it, I could feel my cheeks flushing bright pink.

Evan looked shocked. "Wait a minute. Didn't you say you were going to the dance with Bevan?" When he said "Bevan," he said it like it had quote marks around it.

"Not anymore."

Evan got a funny look on his face. "Maddy, I'm . . . um, sorry. But—"

"Evan, c'mon. You can't be mad at me anymore. I'm practically begging over here."

"No, it's not that. It's just, well . . . I'm kind of going with someone else now." He wouldn't look me in the eye.

GIVE ME A
154!

Tuesday, March 1

Lunchtime, on school steps

Song Level:

Cheer Me a River

At school today, the first thing on my to-do list was to find Evan. As usual, the first thing that greeted me when I walked through the heavy school doors was that stupid poster for the Sunshine Dance. But by now, some kids had already enhanced it by adding doodles of butts and giving the sun a mustache. Normally I'm opposed to vandalism, but given my feelings on the dance at that moment, I kinda got a kick out of it.

I usually can find Evan before first period in one of three places: by his locker, by the snack machine, or waiting by his class. I checked his locker: an empty bag of Doritos, no Evan. I checked the snack machine: an empty bag of Cheetos, but no Evan (hmm . . . could there be a meaning behind this mystery junk-food trail?). Finally, I found him walking down the hall toward me, his backpack slung over one shoulder.

GIVE ME A
153!

bit, so I'll just grab something."

Mom turned to look at me before she walked out of the room. "One more thing. I promise not to embarrass you too much at the dance."

"Yeah, I hope so."

"Don't forget to eat protein!" she shouted behind her.

"Okay!"

It's a good thing Mom always leaves leftovers. All this drama had made me STARVING!

GIVE ME A 152!

"Aha. You're a smooth one, Miss Maddy."

"Like mother, like daughter," I teased.

"So what is the 'other stuff' that's bothering you?"

"Oh. Well, it's the dance."

Mom frowned. "Why? What happened? I mean, other than me crashing it."

I rolled my eyes. "Well, I kind of just dumped my date."

Mom let out a slow whistle. "Ohhh. I see."

"It wasn't working out with us." I shrugged. "Whatever."

(Mom + me) x Boy Talk isn't my favorite equation.

"But you're still going to go to the dance, right?"

"I think so. But anyway, tryouts are what's most important right now."

Mom nodded. "Do you need any help from me?"

I smiled. "Well, I'll need you to, ahem, observe our usual pre-tryout traditions: the Waving of the Pom-Pom. The Picking of the Outfit."

"You got it. And my lips are sealed. I'll be sad to see you leave our team, but this is what you've always wanted. And you're right to go after it. You're gonna be super. Speaking of, you'll need your energy. I'm bringing you some dinner."

"No, no. It's cool. I'm gonna go downstairs and write a

GIVE ME A
151!

like since winter break. But I didn't decide to officially try out until a few days ago."

"And you didn't tell me. Why?"

"Mom, you're my coach."

"I'm your mother. I was your mother long before I was your coach, and I'll be your mother long after. I support you no matter what you decide to do, you know that."

That made me smile. "I know, thanks."

"So, is that really why?" she pressed.

"I guess, maybe, part of me didn't want to disappoint you again. You know, in case I don't make it. So I figured, what you didn't know wouldn't hurt you."

"Oh, sweetie! You could never disappoint me," she replied, pulling me into a big bear hug (ha-ha, I didn't even plan that one!). "You have no idea how proud I am of you. No matter what you choose, I know you'll shine. Besides, you've come a long way as a cheerleader. There's no way they can refuse you now!"

"Thanks, Mom. That means a lot."

"So where have you been practicing?" asked Mom. "I haven't heard you jumping around your room like you usually do before tryouts."

"You won't believe this, but Katie Parker has been training me during the day."

GIVE ME A 150!

"What's really bothering you, Maddy? I know the dance thing made you angry, but you were acting strange before that."

I hadn't told Mom about Titan tryouts. I wasn't sure what she'd say, what with being the Grizzly coach and all. But deep down, that's not really why I held back. It's just, when I didn't make it last time, the look of disappointment on her face was, like, burned in my brain. I know she loves me and wouldn't care if I stayed a Grizzly forever, but I guess I'm just afraid that I'll disappoint her again.

It was definitely weird not sharing it with her, since she's always backed me up on everything cheer related. I decided that since she was feeling a little guilty for ruining my dance, it would be a good time to tell her the truth without her getting too mad at me.

"It's tryouts. And some other stuff."

Mom looked puzzled. "Tryouts? For what?"

"For the Titans."

As the realization hit her, she leaned back on both arms and looked up at the ceiling. Perhaps this is a new yoga pose they call "Oh No She DIDN'T!"

"Sorry, I'm just a little surprised," said Mom. "I can't believe you didn't tell me. When did you decide to try out?"

"I'm sorry. I've been thinking about it for a while,

GIVE ME A 149!

or I might have jumped out the window. I was glad I'd had that convo with Bevan, but it didn't exactly make me feel calmer. I was actually feeling a little guilty, on top of everything else.

"Madison," said Mom, "I know you're not thrilled that I'm going to your school dance."

I rolled my eyes. "Not thrilled? How about <u>mortified?</u>"

"Okay," said Mom. "Fine, mortified."

That was better.

"I knew you wouldn't really be excited. But I'd hoped you'd react a little better to the whole thing."

"Yeah, sorry to disappoint." I was in a grumpy mood and determined to stay that way, no matter how nice Mom was trying to be.

Mom's eyes fell on my dress. She picked it up and held it in front of her. "Wow. This is beautiful! Unbelievable!"

"Thanks," I said.

"You're really something, Madington."

This time I couldn't hold my frown in place. I'm a girl who loves a compliment! What can I say? I can't help it.

"I've been working really hard on it."

Mom touched my knee, signaling that she was about to ask me something I might not want to answer. That's always how she begins her "serious talks."

GIVE ME A
148!

know how to end this convo. It was so hard—for both of us. I'd never, like, dumped anyone before. I knew it was the right thing to do, but for a right thing it felt incredible wrong. Suddenly, I heard someone talking to Bevan. "Dude! You done hiding from us?"

"Yeah, I'll be right there. Maddy, I gotta go."

"Okay. Hey, Bevan?"

"Yeah?"

"I'm sorry too."

"Yeah. Okay, I guess I'll . . . see ya round."

"Yeah. See ya," I said. Although with our track record, I highly doubted I would.

As soon as I hung up the phone, there was a knock on my door.

"Sweetie?" called Mom. "Are you sleeping?"

"No."

"Can I come in?"

I sighed. "Yeah, sure. Why not," I grumbled.

Mom came in, dressed in her yoga pants and tank top. She must have been doing one of her "Sun salutation" videos. She looked pretty zen'd out. Totally the opposite of how I was feeling at that moment.

She did her best to clear a spot on the floor next to me, but had to sweep away piles of thread, fabric, and sequins. Luckily, she didn't comment on the mess

GIVE ME A
147!

lately. And I'm sorry I hurt you. But I thought you of all people would understand. It's not like I'm just goofing off and ignoring you. I'm a hundred percent soccer, twenty-four/seven. You know what it's like to completely commit yourself to something. Soccer is like my cheer."

I appreciated the fact that he was trying to explain, but it wasn't really helping. "Yeah, I'm devoted to cheer, and I understand what that's like. But I make time for the people who are important to me."

"Listen, Maddy. I really like you. Don't you know that?"

Tug on my heartstrings much? Yes, it was cute and sweet and all that. But the second he said it I knew deep down, no matter how nice it was to hear, it was coming too late. "I'm sorry, Bevan. I wish things were like before, but they're not. I just feel differently. About everything." I was thinking about the way that Evan is always there when I need him, and even when I don't. The way he just seems to "appear" outside the gym when I'm leaving practice. "I need someone who wants to spend time with me, and not just when it works out with his schedule."

"Well," he said. "I'm sorry, I can't be that way. At least not during soccer."

We were both silent for a few moments. I didn't

GIVE ME A 146!

"Bevan, I'm sorry, but I can't go to the dance with you."

"What do you mean? Is everything okay?"

He sounded worried, which was cute. But I didn't want to be going out with someone who only paid attention to me if I got hit by a bus or something.

"Yes. I'm fine. Everything's fine. It's just . . . things have been different between us, right?"

Bevan didn't say anything for a few seconds. I was worried I'd have to repeat the words that took so much courage for me to say. "I guess," said Bevan finally. "Actually, what are you talking about? Different how?"

I couldn't believe he hadn't noticed that we hardly hung out anymore and barely spoke to each other at all. Not even in the hallways. Seriously?

"Bevan, the last time we spoke was at Bowl-o-Rama, like, two weeks ago. We hardly see each other. Maybe that doesn't bother you, but it bothers me. And hurts my feelings."

"Wait, hold on." I could hear him trying to muffle the phone as he shouted at his friends. "Guys! Shut up! Maddy, I'm going into another room, hold on. Okay, you there?"

"Yep."

"Okay, yes, that's true. Things have been really busy

GIVE ME A 145!

dress in town (ahem, Clementine) or because it's from some chic boutique in L.A. (yes, you, Hilary). But because I'm making it unlike any other dress out there. It's like the outfits . . . belong together! And who am I to deprive them of their fashionably ever after?

By the time I bit off the end of the piece of thread I'd used to sew the tulle, my mind was made up. I couldn't go to the dance with Bevan. It wouldn't feel right. It wouldn't BE right. I'm just not interested anymore. Maybe it's because he's been so wrapped up in soccer and I know I deserve better. Maybe it's because I'm finally starting to realize that what I feel for Evan is, like, WAY more than you feel for a friend. Even a best friend. But whatever the reason, the choice was clear. FINALLY!

I worked up the courage, dialed Bevan's number, and waited. I wasn't sure he'd pick up. I mean, if he was around, why wasn't he calling to say hi? It'd been forever.

"Hey, Maddy!" he said, when he answered the phone. "Sorry, I only have a sec. What's up?"

I could hear the sound of guys talking in the background. I figured he had some friends over. There wasn't going to be an easy way to say what I was about to say. I would just have to put it out there.

GIVE ME A 144!

just be like normal moms, and not date someone from my school and not go to my dance? We talked about this already, and you promised you'd play it cool. This is not cool!"

I stomped up the stairs to my room, not caring that I would miss dinner. (Besides, I was pretty sure I had a half-eaten bag of M&M's somewhere in my room. Far from gourmet, but it was something.) Now, on top of stressing about tryouts, Bevan, and Evan, I can add this to the list.

I still had some work to do on my dress, and that is always a nice little distraction for me. So I went to work.

Of course, as I was sewing a super-rad layer of tulle under the skirt (volume is so in), I couldn't help but think how great this dress would look next to Evan and whatever old-school look he's going to be pulling off. Most guys at our school will show up in standard collared shirts and ties, and maybe jackets. But Evan's the type to wear his dad's prom shirt and a jacket from the Salvation Army with a pair of jeans and Converses. Sometimes, even though his way of dressing is kinda out there, I think it's better to be unique than to look like everyone else. And my dress is sure to stand out. Not because it's the most expensive

GIVE ME A
143!

you ask? Um, because this is a D-I-S-A-S-T-E-R! Who else but me would have a mom who would willingly go to her daughter's school dance? Doesn't she know how embarrassing this is going to be? Having your mom show up to your school dance is, like, a fate worse than death. I might as well say good-bye to all my friends now. They're not going to want to know me when it's MY mom playing referee at the dance.

Then I realized, this is going to be even worse than I could imagine. My mom isn't like other moms. My mom will probably show up to the dance in a supercute dress, looking like she just stepped out of a Bloomingdale's catalog. All the girls will go up to her and say, "Coach Carolyn, you look stunning!" and all the boys will shyly say hi. She might even be crowned Sunshine Queen and MY LIFE WILL BE OVER.

"Maddy, say something. I know this isn't ideal, but won't it still be fun to get all dressed up together?" Mom was looking at me hopefully.

Uh, if we were, like, going to a family wedding, maybe. But getting dressed for a school dance? That's something you share with friends. NOT YOUR MOTHER!!!

"Ohmigod, Mom. I thought I was having a bad day, but you just made it ten times worse. Why can't you

GIVE ME A 142!

didn't push it when I didn't feel like talking in the car. I put on the radio, and of course a really sad Pink song was playing. Why does that always happen? Why can't I be in a bad mood, turn on the radio, and find my FAVORITE happy song is playing? It feels like a cruel joke.

When we got home, I helped Mom with dinner. We were making a big garden salad and risotto, and I was on salad duty.

Mom and I were both in our own worlds, getting lost in the sounds of cooking. Then she ruined it.

"So, Madington. I have news."

I looked over at her, but she was continuing to stir the risotto in the pot. I knew that lack of eye contact was bad. And whenever Mom announces that she has "news," I can usually assume it's something I won't be too excited about. Like when she told me she and Dad were getting a divorce, she said, "Madington, your father and I have some news."

"Okay," I said, bracing myself.

"I'm going to be at the Sunshine Dance too."

"What?"

Mom put the stove on simmer. "Mr. Datner and I are going to be chaperones together. I hope that's okay."

Um. No. That's, like, the OPPOSITE of okay. Why,

GIVE ME A 14!!

As I waited for Mom to meet me in the parking lot, I saw Evan walking toward me. I waved at him, but he didn't wave back. I thought about going up to him, but I was pretty sure the whole not-waving-back thing was deliberate. I felt terrible. Evan is one of my best friends, and now he's really mad at me. It's not like I want to go back to how we were before I realized I kind of like him. Not at all. I just wish we could go back to how we were at Just Desserts, before the topic of the Sunshine Dance came up.

A minute after my wave got rejected I saw Mrs. Andrews's car pull up to the curb. She saw me and waved (and I waved back, because I'M polite, unlike some people). I could see her asking Evan something, which I assume went something like, "Why don't we offer Maddy a ride home?" Because that's something we would usually do. Evan got into the front seat and sat there, shaking his head. I imagine he replied something along the lines of, "Maddy is an evil siren who ripped my heart out and therefore should be forced to walk forever." But when they drove past me, I DID see him quickly turn to look my way. I don't know what that means, but I'm going to take it as a good sign. Because right now? I need some good.

Mom could tell I was in a bit of a mood, so she

GIVE ME A 140!

finally popped the question last week?"

"Oh, yeah, right." OOPS! I'd been thinking about Katie and totally slipped up. "Well, do you have any prospects?"

"You mean besides Matt, who keeps begging me to go with him? Not so much."

"_what_?" My jaw dropped so low, I'm surprised it's still hinged. "Matt asked you to the dance? How could you _not tell me this_?"

"It's not a big deal," she said nonchalantly. "You haven't really been around lately, so I guess it slipped my mind."

I felt bad about being so MIA. I wanted to tell Jacqui what's been eating up all my time, but obvi I couldn't. I can't wait until tryouts are over already! All this secrecy is exhausting.

"Yeah, sorry about that," I told her. "I've just been really busy. So, Matt has a crush on you, huh. That's cute!"

"Please don't say that," she whined.

"Oh, c'mon. I'm just teasing. So, are you going to say yes?"

"Well, I've been saying no for, like, three weeks, but no one else has asked me and I'm starting to reach a breaking point."

"Okay, well, keep me posted this time!"

GIVE ME A 139!

day before, and Tabitha Sue cheered the loudest.

When everyone was getting ready to leave, Diane took Tabitha Sue by the hand and started pulling her toward Ricky. Tabitha Sue looked a little scared—like she hadn't planned on actually having to talk to the guy.

"Tabitha Sue," said Diane, "have you met my friend Ricky?" Diane deposited a dumbstruck Tabitha Sue in front of Ricky, and I tried not to stare as I watched the two of them talking to each other. Diane left them there and walked back to the group.

"What was that about?" I asked Diane, even though I totally knew the answer.

"Ricky's been wanting to ask her to the dance for, like, ever," said Diane. "He just needed a tiny bit of help."

When Tabitha Sue came into the locker room, she practically did a high kick from being so happy. "I'm going to the dance, everybody!"

Jacqui, Diane, Katarina, and I all cheered for her.

"Hey, Tabitha Sue," said Jacqui. "Can I borrow some of that lip gloss? It looks like your trick worked, and I can use a little help in that area."

"What do you mean?" I asked Jacqui quietly. "You don't have a date either?"

"What do you mean 'either'?" she asked, an odd expression on her face. "Didn't you say that Bevan

GIVE ME A 138!

little effort." She picked up her mascara and started applying it.

"Oh really?" I asked. I knew this had to have something to do with impressing Diane's friend Ricky.

"Yes, really," said Tabitha Sue, concentrating in the mirror. "Isn't looking good part of the whole 'cheer confidence' factor?"

Jacqui spritzed some of Tabitha Sue's hairspray onto her ponytail and turned to walk away. "You're scaring me, Tabitha Sue."

"Me too," I said. "But you look great."

"Thanks," she said. "I'll be right out."

I guess the hair and makeup thing worked, because Tabitha Sue was extra on point during practice. She was practically leading everyone through the dance routine, and helped Ian with some moves he wasn't getting. It was fun to see her so excited and confident. I made a mental note to spend more time than usual making myself up for tryouts. It seems like it works! (At least it can't hurt, right?)

Toward the end of practice, like clockwork, I saw Ricky take a seat on the bleachers closest to us. Tabitha Sue didn't notice at first, but when she did, this huge smile came onto her face.

We went over a new cheer we'd taught the team the

GIVE ME A 137!

snotty, but mainly just had super-annoying friends. Plus, I was obsessed with being as good a cheerleader as my mom was, and not half as focused on being the best cheerleader I can be. Even funnier, I thought people like Jared and Tabitha Sue were total geeks (talk about snotty!). I'm still nervous, but I feel like a different person. Like I have a whole new attitude. Maybe that will make all the difference this time?

LATER THAT NIGHT, ON MY LIVING ROOM COUCH

When we were getting ready for practice, I couldn't help but notice a certain someone (ahem, Tabitha Sue) taking a little longer than usual. Tabitha Sue is usually one of those more laid-back girls, who doesn't obsess over hair and makeup but effortlessly looks cute. So when I saw her break out a makeup bag and multiple hair products, I had to comment.

I sidled up to the locker-room mirror and picked up one of her lip glosses that had rolled away.

"What's up, Maybelline?" I asked.

Tabitha Sue blushed.

Jacqui must have noticed too. "You have a hot date at practice or something?" she joked.

Tabitha Sue got even redder. "No," she said. "I, um . . . I just thought, you know, I'd start making a

GIVE ME A 136!

head cheerleader, she's beautiful, and people just seem to want to be around her. I can just picture all the guys in our class hanging around the halls, pretending to look busy as they wait for their perfect moment to ask her out. She probably doesn't even notice when it happens.

"I hope so," said Katie. "But, more important, tryouts are this Saturday. Can you believe it?"

My heart stared doing loop-de-loops. I swallowed nervously. "No, I can't."

"Maddy, you know what we keep talking about. Confidence! That's your secret weapon on tryout day. If you feel good about yourself, you'll ace any test the judges throw your way."

I smiled. "Working on it."

"I wish I could tell you exactly what drills and things the judges are gonna ask you to do, but I can't."

"Of course you can't!" I assured her. "Cheating is never cool. Besides, if I make it, I want to make it purely based on talent."

We started changing back into school clothes. "Thanks for everything, Katie."

As I headed to class I couldn't get out of my head how different tryouts are this time versus last time. During last tryouts, I hardly knew Katie. I thought that she was, like, Miss Perfect, who was sometimes

GIVE ME A 135!

me guess," she said. "Soccer?"

"Yes!" I said, relieved that I had someone to talk to who really understood. Like, from firsthand experience. "It's, like, all he does! It's all he cares about, it seems."

Katie sighed. "Yep. I've had the joy of experiencing that side of Bevan too. It can get to be really frustrating."

"What did you do about it? If you don't mind me asking, I mean."

Katie chewed on her lip as she thought. "I tried talking to him. I planned things for us to do together. But he just couldn't give it up, not even a little bit. And I guess that's a big reason we broke up."

OMG! Can you believe? It's like he's repeating what happened with Katie with me. And the worst part is, he doesn't even realize it!

"Well . . . ," I said, not sure how to end the conversation. "It's just annoying, I guess." I decided to steer the conversation more to Katie. "And anyway, do you have any more prospects in terms of dates?"

Katie shook her head. "Nope. No one."

"Oh, I doubt it, Katie. I'm sure tons of guys want to ask you. They're just working up the courage." It's completely insane that Katie is having a problem finding a date. It, like, goes against the laws of nature. She's

GIVE ME A 134!

so embarrassing, but I still don't have a date!"

"You're kidding!" I exclaimed, without thinking.

"Gee, thanks a lot, Maddy."

"No, I'm sorry, what I meant is that I figured a girl like you would be the first one with a date. In fact, I thought you'd have trouble fighting them off."

Katie laughed bitterly. "Well, I'm embarrassed to admit it, but I sort of thought so too. But all the guys I thought would ask me ended up asking other girls. So the joke's on me, I guess. Oh, and Clementine and Hilary just won't shut up about their stupid dates."

"Oh, believe me, I get it. Until recently, I was in your shoes," I told her.

"Aren't you going with Bevan?"

"Yeah, but he took forever to ask me."

"You don't seem so excited," said Katie.

I wasn't so sure how much I wanted to tell Katie just then. First of all, Bevan was her ex. Second, we'd gotten into a fight in the past about him.

I guess she could tell I wasn't so into sharing with her, because then she smiled and said, "I promise not to judge."

"Well, Bevan's been kind of weird lately. We hardly talk to each other anymore."

Katie nodded like she'd been there, done that. "Let

GIVE ME A 133!

"Good!" said Katie. "Okay, now do a front hurdler."

I couldn't help but roll my eyes. This was easy stuff (or so I thought).

I reached up high into the air, extending one leg out and bending the other.

Katie was not impressed. "Higher," she said. "It's not enough to be 'good' at these moves. You have to be the best. You need to be the girl at tryouts with the highest front hurdler."

I nodded and tried again.

"Again," said Katie.

We did this for what seemed like forever, and then we went through cheering while smiling and making eye contact. I have no problem with these things when I'm home or with the Grizzlies. But when I think about cheering in front of the judges, I get all JELL-O kneed.

When we were doing our cooldown stretches, I could tell something was bothering Katie.

"Mind if I ask what's wrong?" I said.

Katie looked at me, then shook her head. "It's so stupid."

"You can tell me. I promise not to judge."

She waited a few moments, drawing circles on the floor with her forefinger. "It's this dumb dance. This is

GIVE ME A
132!

she started shaking me! "Maddy! Maddy!" she said over and over again.

When I opened my eyes, I realized I had fallen asleep on the cafeteria table. I had drool on one arm, and when I looked up Katarina was there, looking worried.

"You be all right, yes?" she asked.

Whew. That was some daydream. More like a daymare. This dozing-off thing was getting out of control—even for me. When tryouts are over, I'm going to give myself a full week of going to bed early and sleeping late on the weekend.

"I saw you sleeping wis zee table, so I try to make you awake," said Katarina.

I tried not to laugh. "Um. Thanks, Katarina. Yeah, I guess I need some more sleep!"

"Okay," she said. She didn't look any less worried. "I see you at the practice!"

After two afternoon classes, I met up with Katie in my favorite class of all: Titan training. We stretched for a long time, then Katie drilled me on the harder jumps. I'm still a little wobbly on my pikes.

"You're reaching and dropping your chest too much," said Katie. "Think of it as folding your body in half."

I tried for the tenth time.

GIVE ME A 13!!

bugging out over telling the team you were going to New York during break, and they ended up being cool with it?"

"I know, I know. But this is bigger. Worse. I mean, I know they'll be fine without me if I actually make the team. I just don't want them to think I'm a giant traitor."

"Yeah, I hear ya." Lanie glanced down at her cell on the table. "Listen, let's chat more about this later. I have to stop by the Daily Angeles before class."

"Say hi to your boyfriend for me," I said, batting my eyelashes.

I was going to leave and take a leisurely walk to class, but instead I decided to chill and think about what the Grizzlies will say when I tell them I'm trying out for the Titans. But as usual, me zoning out = daytime nightmares, and I was suddenly pulled into this bad dream where the Grizzlies were at my funeral. But everybody was dancing in the streets and there was a huge jazz band playing around my casket. My whole team was dancing to the music, and they couldn't hear me shouting from inside the casket, "I'm still here! I'm not dead!" Finally, Katarina heard me and opened the casket. Instead of being relieved that I was still there, she pointed a finger at me and shouted, "Traitor!" Then

GIVE ME A 130!

powder blue and from the Stone Age, but come on—
that's so Evan! Right? I thought about what it would
be like to go to the dance with Evan. We'd goof around,
we'd laugh. I wouldn't have to worry about him being
distracted by something else.

"Maddy, you're getting your daydream-y look," said
Lanie.

I frowned. "I'm just really confused."

Lanie handed me an onion ring. "Here, eat this. The
oily deliciousness will solve everything."

I took a bite and savored the crispy, salty coating.
"Mmmm. Okay, problem numero uno solved. I'll be going
to the dance with a big ol' carton of onion rings as my
plus one. Now, onto my problem number two."

"Is your life always this full of drama?" Lanie
teased. "What now?"

"Oh, you know. I'm totally freaking out about tryouts.
Which, by the way, I've finally decided to go to."

Lanie looked at me approvingly. "Really? I'm so proud
of you! This time they better take you—or else! Do the
Grizzlies know?"

I shook my head. "No," I said guiltily. "I haven't had
the heart to tell them. Or maybe I'm just being wimpy
about it."

"You should tell them. Remember you were completely

GIVE ME A
129!

"Our little guy's all grown up. But poor E. You must have ripped his heart to shreds."

I nodded. "I feel awful."

"You don't look so hot either."

"Lanes!"

"I just mean, you look miserable."

"Yeah, well, that's <u>exactly</u> how I feel." I wasn't sure if that was much better, but I let it go.

"So, not to ask the most annoying question ever," Lanie began, "but . . . how does Bevan fit into this equation?"

I sighed deeply. "I think he wants to marry his soccer team. If he hasn't already."

"It's still that bad?" asked Lanie.

"Yeah." I nodded. "I haven't really seen him except for random drive-bys in the hall."

"Ouch. Are you still gonna go to the dance with him?"

Until Lanie asked, I hadn't even thought of NOT going with Bevan as an option. I'd said yes already. Can you un-say yes? He's been so out of touch with me that I started to think maybe that's reason enough to want to tell him I've changed my mind. Who wants to go to the dance with a stranger? Evan has been popping into my head more and more since Saturday night. And when he does, he's always wearing a suit. Sure, it's like

GIVE ME A
128!

other obvious signs I'd been missing.

"Different as in, you used to be able pick a wedgie or burp in front of Evan. Now, every time we're together, you're all self-conscious. Like, smoothing down your hair, and fidgeting with your outfit."

"Lanes, I'm not eleven—I don't pick my wedgie in public anymore. Also, I'm not a truck driver."

"Whatever. You know what I'm talking about. It's kind of . . . obvious."

I was pretty freaked out. I didn't realize that this was all so easy for everyone else to see. I thought I'd hid my feelings for Evan pretty well. Now it turned out I was broadcasting I HEART EVAN in the Daily Angeles.

"Look," said Lanie. "I didn't want to force you to talk about it. I figured you'd come to me when you were ready. So, are you ready?" She wiggled her eyebrows.

I told her everything. About how I was constantly thinking about Evan when I was in New York City. How Luc totally made me realize all the things I like about Evan. How lately, when I picture myself at the dance, the person I'm with IS Evan. And of course, how he asked me on a date THAT I DIDN'T KNOW WAS A DATE! And then to the dance, and how I had to turn him down.

"Awww," said Lanie, putting her legs across my lap.

GIVE ME A 127!

Lanie could tell from the first second we sat down that things were tense between Evan and me.

"Uh, guys? Anything you want to talk about?" Lanie looked from me to Evan and back. "This is almost as bad as the time you dropped Evan's pet hamster," she said under her breath.

"It's nothing," I said.

Evan gave me the LOOK OF DEATH and slammed his glass of milk down on his tray. (Not quite as scary as it could have been, since, you know, it WAS milk and all. But still, quite effective. I jumped.) "I'm out of here."

"You could at least say good-bye!" said Lanie sarcastically. Then she turned to me. "Okay. Spill it."

I thought about it for a split second, and then decided there was no time like the present!

"Evan asked me to the Sunshine Dance."

"I knew it!" Lanie howled. "I knew it, I knew it, I knew it!"

"What do you mean, you knew?"

Lanie took a bite out of a greasy onion ring. "Do you think I'm completely clueless? Wait. Don't answer that. I've noticed how things are kind of different between the two of you."

"Different, how?" I asked. I was curious. I knew I FELT different, but didn't know that there were

GIVE ME A 126!

you at practice, Tabitha Sue,' and then he winked!"
Worry clouded her face. "Do you think he was making
fun of me?"

"No, silly! It's called flirting. Look at the signs! He
was smiling, he went out of his way to say hi to you.
He referenced the fact that he notices you during
practice. And he winked!"

Tabitha Sue blushed. "You think?"

I nodded, smiling. "Tabitha Sue! He totally has a
crush on you!"

Tabitha Sue squealed.

The second bell rang, so it was time for us to get
moving. "See you at practice," I said, with a wink (ha-ha!).
Tabitha Sue turned beet red. Ah, so much to learn.

The morning was okay, but I was DREADING lunch.
It would be the first time I'd talk to Evan since our
date (that I didn't know was a date) on Saturday. I'd
tried to make amends by sending him a text on Sunday,
but he didn't write back. So I knew he must've been
seriously mad at me. It was a bad sitch. I hadn't told
Lanie about what happened, for the usual reasons. The
longer I could avoid telling Lanie about my feelings for
Evan (and vice versa), the longer things wouldn't be
awkward among the three of us.

Boy, was I in for it.

GIVE ME A
125!

Sundays. It's, like, a family tradition," she said with an eye roll. "And my baby brother was being so annoying."

"All right. So your brother was embarrassing?"

"He's always embarrassing. That's not the point. The point is, Ricky was there!"

It took me a moment to process. "Ricky?"

"Diane's friend! From the bleachers. Remember?" said Tabitha Sue exasperatedly.

Ohhhhhh.

"I didn't know his name was Ricky. Sorry."

We rounded the corner to class, and I could tell that Tabitha Sue was on the lookout for Ricky to make sure he wasn't in the hallways.

"That's okay," she continued. "So my brother was singing potty songs he'd learned at preschool at the top of his lungs, and my dad made us finish the parts my brother didn't know. And just as I was saying the word 'pee-pee,' I saw Ricky at the table diagonal from us. He was smiling at me!"

"Wow. Just, wow."

Tabitha Sue fiddled with the hemline of her skirt, keeping her eyes toward the floor. "I know," she said, her voice heavy with embarrassment.

"Well, did he say anything to you?"

Tabitha Sue looked up at me. "Yeah. He said, 'See

GIVE ME A 124!

Monday, February 28

Late afternoon, in the lovely Lounge

Song Level:

Dress You Up

workin' on it!

This morning I was rummaging through my locker, when I heard someone pounding down the hallways. I turned and saw it was Tabitha Sue. And she didn't look happy. She practically had to throw herself against the locker next to mine to slow herself down.

"Whoa, Tabitha Sue, where's the fire?"

She took a few deep breaths. "I had the worst weekend," she moaned. "It was the most embarrassing thing that ever happened to me."

"Wait, back up. What was the most embarrassing thing?"

"Okay," said Tabitha Sue. "Sorry. I'll start from the beginning. Do you have a sec?"

I looked at my watch. Ten minutes till class. "Walk with me."

"My family likes to go to the Pancake House on

GIVE ME A
123!

The whole rest of the way home I could literally feel the anger rolling off his body. He hardly spoke to me. I felt terrible. When we got to my house, he just did this "salute" thing and walked away.

I guess I should have told Evan about Bevan. But I also wanted to tell him that I wasn't really sure I felt anything for Bevan anymore. That I was feeling something . . . for him instead. I almost shouted after him, but the words got caught in my throat. Then it was too late. He disappeared into the night.

Sometimes life is SO unfair.

I went right to my sewing supplies and pulled out my work in progress. I'd taken a break from cheer stuff earlier in the day and gone to sew what to pick out the perfect fabric. This dress might just come along after all. But when I pictured myself wearing it, the guy I was standing next to in my head wasn't Bevan. Yup, that's right. Go ahead and drop that B.

Give me a D-I-S-A-S-T-E-R!

What does it spell? My life.

GIVE ME A 122!

"I don't know what your deal is or anything, but I was thinking, if you don't have a date to the dance, which I don't think you do—"

And I was like, OH NO.

"Wait," I said. I stopped walking and reached out to touch his shoulder. "Evan, I'm <u>really</u> sorry. But I'm going with Bevan."

His eyes widened in surprise, and then he started walking at a fast pace.

"Evan!" I called out, trying to catch up.

He turned to me, an angry look on his face. "I thought you and Bevan were over." He fumbled with the chain that hung from his belt loop to his pocket. "I mean, you haven't mentioned him in, like, a month. And a couple of weeks ago, when we were talking about the dance at lunch, you sounded all bummed about going alone. I just assumed . . . but I guess I was wrong."

He scuffed his shoes against the pavement.

I didn't know what to say. He was totally right. I hardly talk about Bevan at all with Evan. I used to, but then something changed with us, and it just didn't feel right.

"I'm sorry, Evan. If I wasn't going with Bevan, I'd go with you."

"Gee, thanks," Evan huffed.

GIVE ME A 121!

was going to say something else, and little flutters started shooting around in my belly.

But he didn't say anything.

"Thanks," I said. He released his grip from my wrist.

I kept on thinking, "Why is this so weird? We're just hanging out, like we've done a thousand times." Except this time he was all dressed up and ordering for me and staring into my eyes. Then it hit me: WAS THIS A DATE? I couldn't believe it. Was that even possible? And how could I have possibly been on a date with my oldest friend and NOT KNOWN?! I wanted to believe it wasn't true, that I was just hallucinating from all the sugar in my system. But that look on his face—I knew that it meant something more. My stomach fluttered. And yeah, I kind of freaked out.

Then suddenly something shifted, and we were back to just being Evan and Maddy, the BFF version. Maybe he noticed the look on my face and knew the wheels inside my head were turning. Either way, I was a little relieved. Those fluttery feelings are NOT fun—especially when you've just eaten five tons of dessert and you feel like you might barf it all up.

Later, as Evan and I walked back toward our neighborhood, it got quiet again. Evan's hands were in his pockets, and he was staring at the ground.

GIVE ME A 120!

I didn't need to be told twice. I went to shovel it onto my spoon, but I guess I used too much force (who knew I had such brute strength?), because I watched in slow-motion **HORROR** as the chocolate blob landed right in Evan's lap.

"Ohmigod, I'm _so_ sorry!" I leaned across the table to see the damage. It was a big brown blob right on his khaki pants, and it kind of looked like something I don't want to name here. (Hint: rhymes with "moo.")

Evan was dabbing his napkin into water. "Don't worry about it," he said with a laugh. "It happens."

He tried to clean it up, but the stain just spread and looked even worse.

I felt awful. I felt worse than the word that rhymes with moo. "I'm really sorry," I said.

"Seriously, it's fine," he said. I could tell he meant it. I love that Evan doesn't freak out about stuff like this.

"Oh, I have an idea! I'll put some on my lap, and then we'll both look ridiculous." I reached over to grab the napkin he'd grabbed to clean his pants, where inside, the chocolate blob was now totally melted.

Evan grabbed my wrist to stop me. "No, please, don't ruin your outfit. You look so pretty."

Our eyes met, and his hand still held on to my wrist. He was looking at me totally serious now. I felt like he

GIVE ME A 119!

ordering for me is just another step on the weird
ladder we seemed to be climbing.

"I recommend picking different things and then
sharing," she said. And then she winked at us!

Utter MORTIFICATION! Was this woman trying
to ruin my life? I mean, sure I've been a little squirmy
and smiley around E lately, but I've been flying under
the radar. THIS? Is NOT under the radar.

We quickly changed the subject. Evan told me that
his SuperBoy is almost done.

"Does Cupid get his butt kicked in the end?"

Evan shook his head and made the "zip the lips" motion.
"You'll just have to read it, like I said. When it's ready."

"Fine," I said, smiling.

Our plates arrived, and we were completely overcome
by the sugar fantasy that lay before us. There was a
double chocolate fudge brownie, a raspberry parfait, a
giant peanut butter chocolate chip cookie, angel food
cake with strawberry sauce, a plate of bonbons, and a
banana split.

Our absolute fave was the banana split. It had
chocolate, vanilla, and strawberry ice cream in it.
Yummers! When we were down to our last bite of the
chocolate (the best flavor), Evan was like, "You should
have it."

GIVE ME A
118!

curled my hair earlier today so it was still a little wavy. But still . . . if I had known we were playing dress-up, I would have gotten fancier. Hmph.

"Hi," I said. I suddenly felt nervous.

Long, awkward pause.

"So," I said. "How was your day?"

"Good!" he said cheerfully. "How was yours?"

I shrugged. "Looooong day of cheer stuff." I spent the day practicing the moves Katie and I have been doing lately for hours on my lawn when Mom was out doing errands.

"Cool," he said.

A waitress came by wearing an old-fashioned diner uniform: pink collared shirt, little black apron, and her hair in curls. So retro.

"Hey, lovebirds," she said with a wink.

Both of us blushed uncontrollably. I wanted to say, "No, we're not lovebirds, we're just friends," but she didn't give me the chance.

"You want to do the fixed-price menu or à la carte?" She was smacking her gum super loudly.

Evan spoke first. "We'll do the fixed price," he said automatically. Then he looked at me and smiled nervously.

"Uh, sounds good to me," I said, even though Evan

GIVE ME A 117!

Saturday, February 26

Nighttime, in my kitchen, drowning my sorrows in sugar

Song Level:

I Want Candy (and Hot Fudge, and Whipped Cream)!

When I walked into Just Desserts, I couldn't find Evan
at first. I saw this cute guy sitting in a booth at the
far end of the restaurant, but his back was to me. His
hair was perfectly styled, and he had a cute sweater
on. He looked like he COULD be Evan, but, like, in a
parallel universe where Evan dressed cooler and styled
his hair. But then the guy turned around and saw me,
and waved. It WAS Evan! A super-adorable, showered
Evan. Maddy LIKE! When I sat down across from
him, I detected the faint smell of something citrusy.
Cologne? I was like, "Who is this guy?"

"Hey, Maddy." He did one of those looking-me-up-and-
down things, and I immediately wished I had put a little
more effort into my ensemble as well. I mean, I looked
fine and all. I was wearing a long knitted sweater over
skinny jeans with knee-high boots, and I'd actually

GIVE ME A
116!

minute and a button in one hand and a needle in the other. I nearly poked myself in the eye with the needle.

"Phew, close one," I said out loud.

I guess I'm more nervous than I thought.

GIVE ME A
115!

the fall, the more you can anticipate how it is going to feel. As the day of tryouts gets closer and closer, I can't help but feel terrified at how things might go down.

Anyway, after like half an hour of sewing, I must have passed out, because before I knew it I was knee-deep in a horrible nightmare. I'd shown up to tryouts wearing, hands down, the UGLIEST dress EVER. It was like one of those prom nightmare dresses from Mom's eighties movies—the kind in neon colors with ruffles all over and giant pouffy sleeves. And everyone was cracking up, laughing at me. Clementine shouted, "Nice dress!" Even Coach Whipley was clutching her stomach, she was laughing so hard. And Mr. Datner and Mom were both there, and Mr. D told me to do ten laps around the gym for showing up in a dress.

If I tried to do any kind of jump or kick, everyone would see my undies! So I ran to my gym bag and started looking for my shorts and shirt. There was so much in there, but I couldn't find my clothes. It was like digging through the world's biggest laundry pile. But instead of gym clothes, there were just scraps and scraps of fabric.

I woke up with my heart beating a million times a

GIVE ME A
114!

"Don't sweat it," said Lanie. "You can chill with Marc and me."

"Ooh, gotta love being the third wheel."

I glanced at the clock and realized it was getting pretty late. "I gotta go, Lanes. Speaking of the dance, if I don't spend some major time on this dress, I'll be dateless and dressless."

"Well you can only hang with me and Marc if you're wearing clothes," she replied, in all seriousness. "Just giving you fair warning."

"Ha-ha."

One of the things I love about sewing and designing clothes is that it really clears my head. I get into this zone where I just get to focus on the design, and the rest of the stuff in my life fades into the distance. Which was ÜBER nice, while it lasted.

And now that I have to come back to reality, I'm realizing I really need to get my head back into tryouts. It's really happening, and I told Katie I'm going to go for it. Just thinking about what the day will be like makes me feel like I'm on the part of a roller coaster ride where it just keeps inching higher and higher. You know in a few seconds you're going to be free-falling down, but the climbing is so much worse. Because the higher you go, and the closer you get to

GIVE ME A
113!

"Aw, Lanes, he sounds so cute. I love when guys are nervous."

"I know!" Lanie squealed. "Okay, that's the last you'll ever see of 'Excited Lanie.' I hope you enjoyed the show."

"Oh, I sure did," I said, smiling.

"Was Bevan nervous when he asked you?"

"Yeah, he was, just a little. But I don't know, Lanes. He's been MIA since our date on Tuesday. Literally, not a peep."

"Seriously?"

"Yeah. And I'm not going to call him or text him or anything. I'm so tired of it. Why even ask me to the dance if he's planning on ignoring me anyway?" I hadn't realized until just then, as I was talking to Lanie, how upset this has made me. The second I realized it, the rage just grew. "Oh, wait. I just remembered. Yesterday at three thirty he passed me in the hall and punched my shoulder, and then said, 'Later.' Let's set aside the fact that I'm actually not a member of his soccer team and therefore should not be greeted caveman-style— the bigger problem is, there never actually is a later!"

"Oh, Mads. I'm really sorry."

"Yeah, thanks. At least I'm still going to the dance with a date. Even if it's a date who will ignore me."

GIVE ME A 112!

'Sure, why not?' I could have finished the paper at home, but . . .'

"Duh, why would you after that?"

"Exactly. So we were both working, and after a while I got up to go get a soda from the machine. And Marc was like, 'Do you mind if I tag along?' It was funny. I mean, the machine is literally around the corner. It's not like a mile away, you know?"

"Uh, totally!"

"So there I was, waiting for my Dr Pepper to finally roll down to the slot thingy, when Marc just blurted out all at once, 'Are-you-going-with-anyone-to-the-dance?' Like it was one word. Isn't that cute?"

"Supercute. So what did you say?"

"At first I was shocked. No one has asked me to a dance since Mike Pellie the Smellie asked me to be his partner in ring-around-the-rosy in first grade. Then I pulled myself together and said, 'Nah, not really.'"

"You said, 'Nah'?" I repeated, letting her hear the revulsion in my voice.

"Yes. But I followed it up quickly with, 'Are you?' Then he shook his head. And then we stared at each other for a few moments, and then I opened the lid of my soda, which made him finally say, 'Do you want to go together?' And I was like, 'Yes!'"

GIVE ME A
!!!!

being in the car with a very scary version of my mom. Sorry, I wasn't checking my phone."

I could hear Lanie rolling her eyes on the other end of the line.

"So?" I asked.

"Are you ready for this?" asked Lanie. I could hear the excitement mounting in her voice.

"I think so," I said.

"Okay. Your best friend Lanie Marks is going to the dance. Officially! Date and all!" Lanie was in hyper-girlie-girl mode, which I knew wouldn't last long. She hates acting like the teenybopper-type popular girls in our school, who squeal at the sight of a cool skirt. "I mean, it's kind of cool, right?" she said in a more controlled, underwhelmed tone.

"Lanes, it's okay to be excited about this."

"I'm not excited," she said defensively. "I'm just, like, you know, glad that you don't have to worry about me being a dateless loser at the dance."

"Fine, whatever, Lanes. So 'pretend' you're excited, and tell me how it all went down."

"Okay," said Lanie giddily. "We were working after school, and everyone else had already gone home. But Marc and I both had a deadline today, so he was like, 'Are you sticking around a little longer?' and I was like,

GIVE ME A 110!

and **NOT** grossing me out? I miss her dearly 😞.

When we got home, Mom announced that we'd be doing takeout tonight. "Oh, good," I said. "Then can I eat in my room?" I could tell she was a little disappointed that I wouldn't be joining them. She sometimes does this thing where she frowns and rakes her fingers through her ponytail when she's a little upset. But whatever. She's the one who decided to date my gym teacher. I know I said I was happy for her, and I am. But it's complicated. I can't just all of a sudden be BFFs with my gym teacher and want to eat dinner with him and watch movies like we're pals. Weird! She's just going to have to deal with my uneasiness.

I checked my phone to see if anyone had called and realized I'd missed three calls from Lanes. Usually Lanie just calls and leaves a message and waits for me to call her back. Sometimes she'll send a follow-up text. But three calls? Something was up. I hoped it was something good. I needed a little distraction from the blossoming love happening in my kitchen.

"Hey, Lanes, where's the fire?" I asked her.

"Where have you <u>been</u> all my life? I haven't seen you all day!"

"I know, guess we must have missed each other. I've been in a bit of a fog. And I'm still recovering from

GIVE ME A 109!

Mom looked from me to Mr. Datner. "Well, are we all ready?"

We?

"I'm ready," I said, grabbing my bag and hoisting it over my shoulder. Some days it feels like I'm dragging a body in there—it's so full of books, cheer stuff, and who knows what else.

"Here, Madison, let me get that for you," said Mr. Datner.

Excuse me? Is this the same Mr. Datner who orders me to do five laps around the gym for not wearing the right shorts to class? Or the same Mr. Datner who makes us drag punching bags across the floor "for stamina and endurance"? Plus, I wouldn't be caught DEAD letting people see him carrying my bag. Barf.

"No, I'm okay. But thanks."

Mr. Datner looked at my mom, and they made goo-goo eyes at each other. So gross.

The car ride home was almost unbearable. Welcome to Awkward City, population three. Was it really necessary for them to hold hands the entire car ride and giggle like two teenagers IN FRONT OF YOURS TRULY? I really could have lived without it. What has happened to my normal mom? The one who doesn't fall for gym teachers and just stays at home, NOT dating,

GIVE ME A 108!

"They only serve desserts," he explained. "It's like a three-course tasting menu of different dessert-y things."

"Ah, clever title," I said.

"So do you want to go check it out with me? Saturday night?" he asked. His voice squeaked on the word "night."

"Yeah, def!" I said. I **LURVE** dessert. This totally sounds like my kind of place.

Relief washed over Evan's face. "Cool!" he said, getting all fidgety.

Just then I heard Mom's voice drifting down the hall. Then I heard a man's voice. Ugh. Mr. Datner. Not exactly saved by the bell, considering it was Mr. Datner doing the saving.

When the two of them entered the hallway, Evan gave me a look like, "What's going on with those two?" and I just shook my head in a "tell ya later" kind of way.

"Hey," said Evan, nodding hello to Mom and Mr. D.

"I'll talk to you later," I said, hoping Evan would get the hint. I wanted to get out of there, and fast—before anyone else I knew saw Port Angeles's newest lovebirds.

Luckily, he did get the hint, and waved bye. It's nice when you've known someone so long that you don't even need words to communicate.

GIVE ME A 107!

the more likely it is that the person you're lying to will be able to tell you're trying to pull the wool over their eyes. I didn't really care, though. I was glad he'd stopped by.

"Nope, I'm here," I said. I didn't want him to know I was onto him.

"Cool."

"So, um, do you have plans for Saturday night?"

"Just a date with my sewing machine," I answered honestly. "Slaving away on my dress for the Sunshine Dance."

The second the words came out I wanted to grab them and stuff them back.

For a second, I caught him blushing, like the word "dance" triggered something in his brain. And then I was like, "Ohmigod, is he going to ask me about Bevan?" That would ruin our whole, like, groove. Not that I'm purposely keeping the fact that I'm going to the dance with Bevan a secret. I just know that Evan gets all weird about Bevan. I just don't want to upset him, is all. That's nice, right?

LUCKILY he didn't bring up the dance. Instead he randomly started telling me about this place that just opened up in the next town over called Just Desserts and that he was dying to try it.

GIVE ME A
106!

When she turned back toward me, her cheeks were as red as a Red Delicious apple. I stole a quick glance at the guy to see his reaction, and he was blushing while pretending to check his cell phone.

"OMG!" she mouthed to me. I smiled back at her. Awwwww!

NIGHTTIME, BEDFORDSHIRE

After I finished changing in the locker room, I found Evan waiting in the hall. I couldn't help but jump a little bit. For one, I'm used to seeing Bevan waiting for me—though of course that hasn't happened in, like, eons. And second, seeing Evan these days seems to have that effect on me. So crazy!

"Oh, hey, E," I said, suddenly aware that my hair probably looked like a bunch of little birds had been nesting in it for the winter and just flew away.

"Um, yeah," said Evan, running a hand through his own floppy mess of hair. "I was just . . . uh, here late because I was working in the library for a couple of hours on an extra-credit project, and I was passing the gym so I thought I'd stop by and see if you'd left yet."

Uh-huh. Nice try. Because if there's one thing I know about telling a white lie (okay, I'll admit it—I'm kind of an expert), it's that the more detailed it is,

GIVE ME A 105!

"Do you really think we'll do this at the dance?" asked Jacqui, out the side of her mouth.

"Who knows," I said. "I'm kind of hoping we don't. Not because it's not going to be an awesome routine—I just am not into spontaneous dancing. But I can't even think about how sad that would make Jared."

"Oh, totally," said Jacqui.

But by the end of practice, the routine was coming along so well, a big part of me started hoping we do end up showing it off at the dance. Either way, the Grizzlies now have some extra moves under their belt to show off at the Get Up and Cheer! competition that's coming up.

As we did our cooldown, I noticed Diane's friend had taken a seat on the bleachers. And he was STARING at Tabitha Sue—there was no denying it.

I locked eyes with Tabitha Sue and tried to tell her without saying anything that "he" was there. At first she looked at me like I was crazy or something. Which I don't really blame her for—it sort of looked like I was challenging her to a blinking contest. But finally I was like, "Ahem" and did this throat-clearing thing, and nodded my head ever so slightly toward the bleachers. She didn't even pause before whipping her head around to see what I'd been trying to get her to look at.

GIVE ME A
104!

"You guys are just insecure in your masculinity," said Jared.

He was obviously bummed that the shimmy-to-the-floor bit he'd come up with had been rejected unanimously.

"I have to agree with Ian," said Matt, ignoring Jared's comment. "We've gotta draw the line somewhere. I am not doing any hip shaking."

"Your hips don't lie," joked Ian.

"Okay, we promise not to make anyone feel like they look stupid or do anything that makes them uncomfortable at the dance," said Jacqui.

"Ahem," said Jared. "I think 'stupid' and 'uncomfortable' are subjective terms here. No one seems to appreciate any of my stellar additions to the choreography. Doesn't anyone here have taste?"

Tabitha Sue giggled. "Yeah, but I think as a group we tend to prefer Step Up to Flashdance."

"It's Footloose," said Jared, rolling his eyes.

"At least we're doing a dance, right?" said Tabitha Sue, seeing that Jared was a little upset. She's always such a good peacemaker.

"I guess . . ."

We added a few more steps of choreography, then Jacqui and I stood back to watch them run it through.

GIVE ME A 103!

Ian looked stunned. "You could do that?"

"Of course," said Mom with just a hint of smugness. She must have been seriously bugged about Ian's lack of dedication to threaten that. Sometimes she forgets that part of being a cheerleader is having fun, too. But I wasn't going to defend Ian. No way.

"If you don't show yourself as a committed, serious team member, then how do you expect your coach to want you back on his football team?"

Ian let this sink in a little. "I'm sorry, Coach," he said. "I guess I got a little carried away." Whether he actually meant that or he just knew what lines to say, I'm not quite sure.

"Apologize to your captains as well," she said, nodding toward Jacqui and me.

Ian let his head hang. "I'm sorry, Jacqui. I'm sorry, Maddy."

"Are you ready to do this again, minus your stink?" said Jacqui.

"Ready, I promise," he swore.

Everyone assembled back into formation. "You guys ready for more choreography?" I asked.

"Listen," said Ian. "I swear I'll stop goofing around, but just so you know, I am not doing any girly dancing moves. It's not in my contract."

GIVE ME A
102!

"Seriously, dude, you need to take something for that," said Matt.

Mom walked over to where Jacqui and I were standing. "I think that boy needs a good talking-to," she said.

"More like a smackdown," said Jacqui. "Ian!" she barked. "Get your smelly butt over here. Now."

"Hey, Cap'n, you sure you want to do that?" He continued to wave behind his butt like the smell was still coming out and he wanted to better share it with the rest of the room.

"Yes, I'm sure."

For a second Ian's cat-that-ate-the-canary grin faded, but when he looked at Matt, he made sure to plaster it on again.

"What seems to be the problem, ladies?" said Ian.

Before Jacqui could say anything, Mom stepped in. Which probably was better, because Ian knows not to push it too far when it comes to adult authority.

"Your behavior is completely unacceptable," said Mom, stone-faced.

Jacqui and I nodded emphatically.

"Just in case you weren't aware," Mom continued, "I have the power to decide whether you ever return to the football team or not."

GIVE ME A 101!

much stronger this time around. And you're a better cheerleader. You have way less to be nervous about. It won't happen this time."

I'm sending a little prayer to the cheer gods that Katie is right.

Off to practice!

POST PRACTICE, THE NOT-SO-COMFY LOCKER ROOM BENCHES

Everything was going smoothly until Ian let out a loud fart when the choreography called for the guys to catch the girls mid-fall and pull them through their legs. Katarina was Ian's partner, and just as he pulled her through, he totally let one rip. Katarina stumbled and fell flat on her butt.

"Vat is dees smell?" she exclaimed, half gagging.

At that point, the smell hit the rest of the team, and we must have looked hilarious to anyone watching, because all of a sudden we were running left and right, waving our hands in front of our faces to get rid of the smell.

Ian just stood there, hand on his hips, with a triumphant grin on his face. "Ahhh," he said, smiling. "Hamburger with onions for lunch! Hey, can we add this to the routine?"

GIVE ME A 100!

sing it in my sleep. It's not complicated at all—but my memories of how badly I messed up at the last tryouts got the better of my nerves.

"C'mon," said Katie. "Dig deep. You know it."

I shook my head like a deer in headlights.

"Madison, don't do this. I know you have it in you."

I took another one of those yoga breaths and concentrated. I knew this. I KNEW THIS!

And moments (which felt like eons) later, it came to me:

> IF YOU'RE NOT A TITAN
>
> GET OUT OF HERE!

And on the "out" we would pretend to shove a cheer partner in the shoulder. The partners would pretend to stumble backward, but instead do backflips and transition into the bases of a pyramid.

(I think this cheer is supercute to the nth degree. Those Titans know what they're doing.)

When I was done, I felt like such a failure. With a capital F. If I can't remember a single stupid cheer, how the heck am I going to ace tryouts?

Katie gave me a pat on the back. "Chill. You're just nervous, that's all. You made a big decision today."

"Yeah, well, nerves are what got me the last time."

Katie looked me dead in the eye. "Yeah, but you're

GIVE ME A
99!

about her tryouts, I did everything I could to psych her into walking into auditions with all the confidence in the world. If I'm so good at doing that for other people, why am I so lousy at doing it for myself?

"Thanks, Katie. I don't know what I'd do without you."

"Well," Katie began, "you'd probably have a lot less aches and pains, for one thing."

"True." I laughed.

Katie did her best to simulate the tryouts from last season—we did the same dance routine, cheers, and tumbling sequences. "I studied my notes last night about last year's tryouts!" she winked.

In the middle of one of the cheers, I completely blanked on what came next.

I was like:

> WE ARE THE BEST
>
> WE CAN'T BE BEAT
>
> SO CLAP THOSE HANDS
>
> AND STAMP THOSE FEET
>
> THE TITANS ARE HERE
>
> TO BRING THE CHEER
>
> UHH . . . BLAH BLAH BLAH???

And then I just stood there with my arms in a V, not sure what came next. Which is so ridiculous, because I've said this cheer so many times I can

GIVE ME A 98!

Katie nodded. "Yeah, but it doesn't matter. I feel like you're holding back a little in our practice sessions, and I think it's because you haven't fully committed to trying out."

I hadn't really noticed that at all. In fact, I thought I'd been giving everything I have to give. But that's exactly why Katie is coaching me. Because no matter how good you are at something, you can't coach yourself. And it's precisely for reasons like this. There are just always things about yourself that you can't see. And me holding back is apparently one of them.

"I'm sorry, Katie. I guess tryouts seemed so far off, I keep thinking I have time to decide. But you're right, they're almost here. It's time."

"So are you in?"

"Yes."

Katie must have seen the terrified look on my face, because she reached out and patted my knee. "You're gonna do great. I'm right behind you in this."

I nodded.

"Hey, remember how you psyched me up for my tryouts for dance school when we were in New York? I'm going to do the same for you. I know you're going to make it."

Again, she was right. When Katie was worried

GIVE ME A 97!

I'm going to end up going in jeans!!

Finally I snapped out of it and I told myself: Be calm. Breathe deeply. Ommmmmm. (I learned this stuff from one of Mom's yoga DVDs.)

And then I felt a tiny bit better.

Luckily, I knew practice with Katie would take my mind off of dresses from L.A. and US Weekly. There's not much time or energy left to think of anything else when you're pushing your body to its limit. I met her in our usual place.

Katie took a seat on the floor, crossing her legs into a pretzel with both knees flat on the floor, as if it took no effort at all.

Uh-oh, I wondered, did I do something wrong?

"Seriously, how do you do that? I have to, like, force my knees down to get them to do that."

I took a seat next to her, trying to copy her pretzel. But it was a major F-A-I-L.

She shrugged like it was nothing.

"What's up?" I asked her.

"Well . . . I know you still haven't made a final decision about whether you're trying out for the Titans, but the truth is, tryouts are just over a week away. It's kind of do-or-die at this point."

"But isn't sign-up not until next week?"

GIVE ME A 96!

disgust. "what about you? Did you decide what you're wearing yet?"

"My mom and I are gonna take a quick trip to L.A. this weekend to find something cute. Nothing I've found so far does anything for my petite frame." Hilary ran her hands along her teeny waist to illustrate her point. Barf.

"Don't you just looooove L.A.?" said Clementine excitedly. "I bought so much stuff there last year when I went with my aunt."

"I know. It's all très chic."

As I listened to the two of them compliment each other (and tried not to barf), my heart started beating nervously. And these horrible, scary thoughts started crowding my mind: What if my dress S-T-I-N-K-S? What if it turns out so bad, an Abby Lincoln kitten sweatshirt looks better than my dress?

My brain went into a total downward spiral. Maybe I've taken on too many things at one time. I haven't even gone fabric shopping yet! What if I end up slaving away every night until the dance, and then have zero energy for tryouts? Do I need a backup plan in case my dress turns into a MESS? Ahhhhhhh! I can't NOT go to the dance now that Bevan finally asked me. But if this dress ends up being a disaster,

GIVE ME A 95!

sure what's gotten into him, but I'm liking it."

Evan considered this. "Hmm, shall we bet on it?"

"You're on. Stakes?"

"I'll let you know later. I'm gonna think about it," he said with a smile.

On the lunch line, Clementine and Hilary were standing in front of me, which is kind of a miracle because they almost never order from the cafeteria. They usually go to the special canteen that you have to pay extra for and get salads that they eat without dressing. Yuck. It's especially out of character because today's Hamburger Day (a GOOD day in the cafeteria, if you ask me). I couldn't help but overhear their conversation, because they were practically shouting. And of course they were talking about the Sunshine Dance and how hot they were going to look.

"I saw my dress on Mila Kunis in US Weekly," bragged Clementine. "Isn't that awesome?"

"You're gonna make Mila Kunis look like she was wearing a garbage bag."

Clementine batted her eyelashes playfully. "You're too kind." She paused before adding, "Just kidding. You're totally right. I'm gonna rock that frock."

"Wasn't it the most expensive dress in the store?"

"Duh, of course!" said Clementine, with a hint of

GIVE ME A 94!

is, I have no idea what's going on, but what I do know? There's **NO WAY** I'm going to have that talk with Evan, of all people.

"Earth to Madison," Evan said in a singsong voice.

"Oh, sorry," I said. "Zoned out for a bit."

"Not even remotely surprising. So, you were about to tell me what you've been up to lately?" Evan asked.

"Oh, lots of cheer stuff. Want to hear a secret?" I asked him.

Evan gave me a little mischievous smile that made my heart flutter in my chest. "You know how much I love gossip," he said sarcastically.

I told him about how the Grizzlies are planning on doing a surprise dance routine at the Sunshine Dance.

"You're joking," said Evan.

I shook my head.

"Well, that's as good a reason as any for me to go, I guess. I need to see this for myself! Ian and Matt— they're doing it too?"

"Well, they're preparing for it. But they haven't agreed to do it at the actual dance. Not yet, anyway."

"That sounds more like it."

"I have a feeling they'll change their minds when the time comes. Those guys are a bunch of show-offs. And honestly, Matt's been pretty cooperative lately. Not

GIVE ME A 93!

"It's good!" I told him. I slid down the wall to sit next to him.

"Thanks."

He looks especially cute today, wearing a red-and-black-checked flannel—which, as usual, is one size too small for him—with the cuffs rolled up. I'm sure E doesn't know that flannel is ACTUALLY in. This is just another hand-me-down.

"So, what's been going on?" he asked, putting his sketchbook away.

I thought of telling him about tryouts for the Titans, but then that would lead to me telling him about Katie training me, and I just really don't like talking about Katie with Evan. Then I started wondering if he and Katie still hang out. Not, like, in a "dating" sort of way. They're definitely only on "friend" terms. Still, the idea that he might be chilling with her gives me an icky feeling in my stomach. But I didn't want to ask because then it would seem like I'm jealous of their friendship in some way. Which I'm not. Obvs. Okay, fine, maybe a little. In that moment I almost decided to ask him anyway, but then my brain spun into, like, a total whirlwind—as soon as I began to speak, I realized that my asking him about Katie could lead to him to asking me about Bevan. WHICH TOTALLY CANNOT HAPPEN. The truth

GIVE ME A 92!

together. I can't believe we're back to this again. He hasn't even texted me to see how I'm doing. It's like he thinks he can take me out for a fun night every now and then, and that in between I can just replay those "dear" memories of our time together over and over again in my head. I bet he thinks nothing is wrong, either.

So for the last few days, when I'm practicing an especially hard jump, I've been picturing Bevan's face when my feet fly into the air. I know, not very nice of me, but I'm angry! By the time we go to the Sunshine Dance, we'll practically be strangers.

When I left Mr. Hobart's class, my brain was so focused on my annoyance at Bevan that I almost tripped over Evan, who was on the floor of the hallway, doodling in his sketchbook.

"Working on SuperBoy?" I asked.

He looked up at me, slightly startled. "I didn't see you coming," he said.

"Yeah, I'm sneaky like that." I smiled.

Evan held up the sketch he'd been working on. "Check it—it's the Cupid story."

In the sketch, SuperBoy was chasing Cupid around the school hallways until he finally catches up to him and steals his arrows.

GIVE ME A 911!

skirt. Like she'd just touched moldy bread or a dirty toilet seat. Ew.

I made sure Mr. Hobart was too involved in singing the praises of the isosceles and—better yet—drawing something on the blackboard before I started the noisy process of unfolding the letter. Mr. Hobart has ears like a hawk and at the slightest rustle, he's been known to zone in on you with his beady little eyes and demand that you read the note out loud to the class.

Slowly, carefully, I unwrapped the millions of little folds. Katie must be an origami whiz or something. Finally, I saw her message, and it was so short I thought maybe there was more I was missing on the back. All it said was "get ready."

Get ready? I felt like in our recent training sessions, we've already gotten to "ready." Lately my body's been hurting so much from overtraining (with Katie, with the Grizzlies, at home on my own), I feel like an old person. Every time I get up or sit down, some part of my body cries out in pain. But Katie's note hinted that this isn't even the worst of it! Might as well start writing my epitaph.

On the other hand, I'm glad that tryouts are on my brain in a BIG way because (surprise, surprise) I haven't heard from Bevan since our bowling night

GIVE ME A 90!

Friday, February 25
Afternoon, outside the gym
Song Level:
get ready
stairway (or pyramid?) to Evan

This morning during math (in between learning about isosceles triangles), I felt a tap on my shoulder. I turned around and it was Clementine. She'd snuck up to my seat while Mr. Hobart wasn't looking. But seriously, Clementine, of all people! I can't remember the last time she said something directly to me that wasn't followed by a snotty look or smirk. I oh-so-casually turned around to see what she wanted. She was holding a note folded into a square maybe the size of my fingernail.

At first I was like, "What would Clementine have to say to me in secret? She's usually more than happy to insult me out loud." Then I noticed Katie behind her, who winked at me. Aha. The true note-giver revealed!

This made a ton more sense. Especially since after Clementine handed it to me, she made a big show of making a disgusted face and wiping her hands on her

GIVE ME AN 89!

going to the dance, and I'm **NOT** going alone. I started to flip through the sew what catalog and consider different types of sequins and fabrics for my dress. There are some totally barf-inducing sequins that look like the kind Mom had on her jean jackets from the Stone Age.

She told me that she used to use something called a "Bedazzler" to add sequins to her clothes. Apparently, at the time, it was considered a "must-have." Well, I don't know where I get my knack for fashion design, but it's **DEFINITELY** not from her.

Gah! It's two in the morning! I have to go to sleep ASAP or I'm going to be going to the dance looking more like a zombie than a fashionista.

GIVE ME AN 88!

"Well, it's not <u>that</u> cool. I really wish you weren't dating someone from school."

"I know, honey. It must be a little strange for you to see him here."

I nodded. "But I <u>am</u> happy that you're happy."

Kind of. It's great when Mom's in a good mood (makes my life easier), but still, can't she be like a normal mom and meet someone at a dinner party or coffee shop? Or on the Internet?

Mom put her cup down to give me a giant bear hug.

"You're choking me!" I joked.

"All right, all right. Just wanted a tender moment with my Madington."

"Yeah, do <u>not</u> call me that in front of Mr. Datner, please!"

"You got it."

I went upstairs to my room to see if anyone was online, but no one was. (Okay, if I'm being honest, the "anyone" I was looking for was Evan.) I saw the patterns and designs I've created for my dress sprawled out on my desk and felt a thrill go through me—now I'm actually creating something that I'll get to wear. There was a part of me before that was worried I'd make this awesome dress and then not have the guts to wear it to the dance by myself. But it's official now—I'm

GIVE ME AN 87!

But what she talked about instead was WAY
WORSE. Like the difference between a cake made of
dirt and a cake made of dog poo. Both bad, but one is
MUCH more disgusting.

"Did you have fun with your friend?"

Why do older people always refer to a kid's
boyfriend or girlfriend as a "friend"?

Ugh. I took the tea bag out of my mug and brought
it up to my face to inhale the steam. "Yeah. I kicked his
butt bowling."

"Good job," said Mom with a smile. "Glad you didn't
lose your bowling skills after all these years."

"Like riding a bike."

I was waiting for her to dig more, but instead
she said, "You know, speaking of dates, I have a date
with Ed this Friday." I could tell from the way she
said it that she was waiting for a reaction from me.
I was glad she seemed so happy lately, but still . . .
Mr. Datner? Oops, I mean Ed. Yep, school will never be
the same. Once word gets to the streets, it will be
O-V-E-R for me.

But instead of telling Mom that this is THE
WORST idea in the world, I just said, "That's cool."
Because I was feeling generous.

Mom looked up at me from behind her cup. "It is?"

GIVE ME AN
86!

Lincoln will have to sit on the bleachers without me.
(Aw, poor gal.)

I excused myself to use the ladies' room, and took
that opportunity to text Lanes. "Guess what, chica? Urs
truly will NOT be an old spinster @ the dance after all!"

"Go grl!" she wrote back.

I put some more lip gloss on and fixed a cowlick
before heading back out.

As I walked back to Bevan, I saw that he was
grinning ear to ear. Guess I made his night? Maybe the
rough times with Bevan will all be over now. Maybe he
realized that he was acting really uncool these past few
weeks and is ready to turn over a new leaf. Like, now
that we're going to the dance together, things might go
back to what they were before with us. Maybe?

And maybe my feelings for Evan will find some way
to hide themselves inside my brain. And stay there.
Because that whole mess is just too confusing. Hmph.

Disaster struck when I got home. Mom asked me
if I wanted some tea, so I was like, "Sure." I hoisted
myself on the counter while we waited for the water to
boil. Mom was acting a little weird, so I was hoping she
wasn't planning on asking what happened on my date. I
would have barfed up those fries Bevan and I shared in
between games.

GIVE ME AN
85!

Or maybe that he needs to focus on soccer right now, so he probably shouldn't see me anymore?

"Do . . . do . . . do you have a date for the Sunshine Dance yet?"

Oh sweet relief! FINALLY! Little cheerleader angels did backflips and loop-de-loops over my head. It was like the roof of Bowl-o-Rama opened and rays of glittery sun were floating through. At this point, this was nothing short of a miracle!

But of course I didn't want Bevan to see my excitement. "Nope," I said, looking off to the side like I was distracted by, I don't know, someone's bowling shoe.

"So would you like to go with me, you think?" he asked shyly.

"Yeah, we could do that," I said. Even though I was annoyed that it took him a century to ask me, I couldn't help but be happy that he asked.

"Awesome," said Bevan, looking relieved.

Seriously, I will just never understand boys. If he was so totally set on going with me to this dance, why didn't he ask me earlier? Why was it on his mind NOW but not, like, a week and a half ago? Is there some weird switch in his brain that puts all Maddy thoughts aside until he actually sees me? So confusing. But more important: Yay! I have a date to the dance! Abby

GIVE ME AN
84!

want to give a go at cheerleading."

Bevan backed away with his hands up in protest.
"Yeah, that's not happening either."

By the end of the game, Bevan had actually learned
to hit a few pins, which we decided was reason to
celebrate. "Soda time?" he asked.

I nodded. It's so weird that when we're together,
Bevan is all eyes on Madison. But when we're not, or
especially at school, it's almost like we're strangers. I
don't get it. Ugh.

Anyway, we went over to the snack bar, which for
some reason always smells more like feet than the rest
of the bowling alley. I got us a seat on one of the high
tables with the swivel-y stools (love those!), while Bevan
got the drinks.

"Hope you like cherry Coke?" he said, holding one of
the cups out to me.

"How did you know?" I said with a smile.

Bevan took a few sips of his drink and then fell
silent. I was a little worried that all of a sudden he'd
gotten bored with our date or something, but then he
looked up at me through that cute little hair curl.

"So, I was wondering . . . ," he said, trailing off.

I waited, not sure where this was going. Was he
going to tell me he thought we should just be friends?

GIVE ME AN 83!

"You good?" Bevan asked.

I shook the clouds of memories from my head. "Yeah, I'm great."

Bevan got us shoes, and I picked out a ball for me and a ball for him. I figured he would need something a little heavier.

Bevan hadn't been lying—bowling was not his strong suit. I got a strike on my first bowl, but Bevan's went to the gutter within seconds of hitting the floor.

"Pay attention," I said. "Because you're about to get schooled."

Bevan laughed. "Oh yeah?"

I motioned for him to come over to where I was standing in the lane. "Do what I do. Hold the ball to your heart, and as you take a few steps, extend your arm down to your side, swing back, and just when you take your last step, swing it forward. But straight!"

Bevan looked like a deer in headlights. "That's a lot of steps. I didn't realize it was that complicated."

"It's not," I said. "It sounds like a lot, but eventually it becomes second nature. Like anything new, right?"

Bevan narrowed his eyes into a mock glare. "Maybe we should play soccer together sometime. Then we'll see how slick you are."

"Ha-ha," I said. "Not a chance. That is, unless you

GIVE ME AN 82!

leaning against the column by the entrance with this one curl falling in his eyes.

"Have fun, sweetie!" Mom yelled out the window.

Cringe.

As I approached him, Bevan's smile grew wider and wider. "Wow, you look great," he said.

I looked down at my outfit. Yay, fashion sense! "Oh, this old thing?" I joked.

He gave me a big bear hug (which was nice) and led me into the bowling alley. I've always loved Bowl-o-Rama. Mom, Dad, and I used to go on weekends when I was little. We'd get three hot dogs with chili on top and two giant sodas while we waited for our lucky lane (aka lane 15) to open up. I don't know why we called it "lucky," because it wasn't like we all bowled amazingly each time, but one day Dad bowled especially well and before we knew it, his lucky lane became everyone's lucky lane. We got so good that we even bought our own bowling shoes that matched (too bad I'm twice that shoe size now). We were Team Hays at the family night bowl-offs.

As soon as we walked in, I turned my head toward lane 15, curious to see if it was free. I sighed. It wasn't. And since it was evening, the place was packed. We'd have to eat, like, five chili dogs to wait for it to be free.

GIVE ME AN 8!!

Hmm . . . what goes with stinky, old, never-been-washed bowling shoes?

I decided to go for a laid-back look with an edge (it is bowling, right?) and chose a tank top with my leather jacket and skinny jeans.

Mom was very annoying the whole ride, trying to pry into my social life. I mean, not like I'm Miss Party Girl or anything, but I guess the fact that I was meeting a boy at the bowling alley was somewhat intriguing to her. HOWEVER, she hasn't exactly been an open book about Mr. Ed "Phys Ed" Datner. And when I tried to bring it up, she just waved me off like, "Oh, well, we're having a good time." (Thanks for that, but seriously? TMI.) What I really want to know is, are they actually dating? Or is this going to be a short-lived thing? That way I can prepare my major offensive against the taunts I'm sure to receive at school.

Well, two can play at that game. When Mom asked me how things were going with Bevan, I just said "Okay" and left it at that. Besides, what girl wants to talk about boy stuff with her MOM? Super yuck. Jacqui is so lucky—her mom would NEVER ask her about stuff like this.

When we pulled up to Bowl-o-Rama, Bevan was waiting for me outside. He looked kind of James Dean-ish,

GIVE ME AN 80!

I crossed my heart. "No, I swear! I didn't put it together till now. Do you think he's cute?"

Tabitha Sue gave an emphatic head nod. "He's adorable! But there's no way he's looking at me."

"Tabitha Sue! You think I'd lie to you?"

"No," she admitted.

"It's true. He does, and he's been coming more and more often."

"Yeah, he's probably coming to look at all the other girls."

"Don't underestimate yourself. Anyway, we should get back to practice, but think about what I said."

I could see Tabitha Sue's mood had definitely gotten better. She even smiled through our mile run around the gym.

Go me! And my powers of bringing happiness to others. Now, how do I bring some happy to yours truly?

THAT NIGHT, ON MY LOVELY FLOOR (COVERED IN SCRAPS!)

So, after practice, I jetted home to get ready for my bowling date with B. I took the quickest shower known to mankind and blow-dried my hair. T.G. it wasn't humid today. I spent a couple of hours (okay, minutes, but they felt longer) agonizing over what to wear.

GIVE ME A
79!

Boy, do I feel Tabitha Sue's pain. But she's taking it way harder than I am.

"You know, I'm probably gonna go by myself too. If I go at all."

Tabitha Sue's eyes nearly bugged out of her head. "You? But you're a cheer captain! Aren't you going to go with Bevan Ramsey?"

I shook my head. "He hasn't asked me."

For the first time during practice today, Tabitha Sue smiled. "Don't worry. He will, I'm positive. Besides, I don't want you to be alone at the dance like me. I mean, it would be nice to have company, but I wouldn't wish it on anyone."

I couldn't believe it. I had set out to make her feel better, and she ended up being the one to comfort ME.

I gave Tabitha Sue a big hug. "You should really have more confidence in yourself, Tabitha Sue. You're an awesome person."

And then something dawned on me.

"Wait a minute," I said. "You know that guy who sometimes waits for Diane during practice?"

"Yeah," Tabitha Sue said, nodding. "What about him?"

"Well, while he's waiting on the bleachers, I see him checking you out."

"You're joking," she said, blushing.

GIVE ME A 78!

it wouldn't be that obvious, and Tabitha Sue slunk over.

"What's the matter?" I asked.

At first she didn't answer. She looked down at the floor, and then back over to the Grizzlies.

"You don't have to talk about it if you don't want to," I assured her. "But you just look so unhappy, and Jacqui and I are concerned."

Tabitha Sue took a deep breath. "No, it's fine. It will be good to get this off my chest. It's just . . . I'm so tired of everyone talking about this stupid dance! And their stupid dates! Katarina and Diane are going on and on . . ."

I couldn't help but cut her off. "Wait, Katarina has a date too? Who?"

It's not like I don't think Katarina is date-worthy (far from it, she's drop-dead gorgeous), but the language thing hasn't exactly catapulted her to the top of the popularity ladder. Most of the time, unfortunately, people pass her in the hall and do imitations of her accent under their breath. So immature.

"A family friend, but I heard he's really cute," Tabitha Sue said miserably. "And Diane is going with Peter Collins. I'm gonna be the only one all alone there." A tear slowly crawled down her face. "Like a giant loser."

GIVE ME A
77!

need my (totally fictional) rich parents to give me
thousands of dollars for shopping sprees. BUT if
I want this dress to actually happen, I have to get
cracking. I mean, I know there's a possibility that I
won't go to this dance at all, but just in case, I need to
be prepared. And I know that whatever I make will be
completely original. In fact, it will be so original it will be
RIDIC! (Ha-ha.)

POST PRACTICE, WAITING FOR MY RIDE OUTSIDE

Not long after I got to practice, I noticed
something was DEFINITELY wrong with Tabitha Sue.
And I don't mean her usual nervous, insecure stuff. She
looked downright sad.

She dragged her feet all during our warm-up, and
she had that look on her face like she was about to
cry. Jacqui noticed too, and we both looked at each
other like "Huh? What's up with her?" When I heard
Tabitha Sue sniffle, I told Jacqui I was going to take a
small time-out to talk to her.

"Good idea," said Jacqui. "G'luck!"

"Hey, Tabitha Sue, can you help me with something?"
I asked. I didn't want to draw attention to the fact
that I was singling her out. Also, I'm slick like that ☺.

I stood in a corner of the gym by the bleachers so

GIVE ME A
76!

"I dunno, guys," said Melanie, who was flipping through a Vogue magazine. "I think we should hightail it to the mall. There's way more variet-ay."

(PS—One of their favorite things to do is to add an "ay" to as many words as possible.)

Lisa rolled her eyes. "Ew, the mall? Gross."

"I wouldn't be caught dead with a mall dress," Yvonne huffed. "Mel, did you take too much cold medicine or something?"

"Guys, relax," said Melanie, obviously flustered. "I was totally just joking. Wow." She slammed her locker shut for emphasis, I think.

As the trio walked away, I could still hear them talking about the "ridic" dresses they were going to buy in this totally casual way, like the way that Lanie and I might talk about buying a new lip gloss. And even though I know that acting the way those girls do and taking what they have for granted is absolutely disgusting, a part of me is definitely a wee bit jealous because (a) if they are shopping for dresses, then it is VERY likely that they have dates (grrrr!), and (b) they probably have enough money to buy five dresses each (I know, I shouldn't care about that stuff, but still . . .).

As I walked to class, I reminded myself that I LOVE, LOVE, LOVE making my own outfits. I don't

GIVE ME A 75!

and think about the dance. I wonder what's taking up all that space in his brain. . . . There sure isn't room for me or the dance, it seems.

I really might be forced to go to this dance alone! I'll be branded a Super Geek for the rest of the year. Or worse: forever!

Things kind of continued to go downhill after that realization. (What else is new?) I was at my locker, getting books for my next class, when I couldn't help but overhear a bunch of girls practically hyperventilating over the shopping spree they plan on taking this weekend. I looked over to see who it was, and was not surprised. Lisa Frankel, Melanie Talbot, and Yvonne Brooks all wear the same clothes, do their hair practically the same, and talk the same.

"Fer real," said Lisa, with a toss of her wavy blond hair. "We're so totally gonna scope out Cecily's Attic first. It's gonna be so ridic!" Her eyes were so wide that it looked like they might pop out of their sockets.

I've actually never been inside Cecily's Attic. It's one of the most expensive stores in Port Angeles. People mainly go there to buy dresses for bat mitzvahs or Sweet Sixteens, but not just for ordinary school dances. Unless, of course, you're oozing money like these girls are.

GIVE ME A
74!

more like he just lets other things be more important than me."

Lanie raised an eyebrow. "Sounds not nice to me."

I nodded thoughtfully. "Yeah, I guess. But the good news is he did ask me to go tonight instead. It just, you know, took him a while to do the right thing."

"So are you going?"

"Yeah, why not, right?"

Lanie smiled. "Sure. But more important, did he ask you to the Sunshine Dance yet?"

I sighed, and shook my head. "But you know, it's cool." I playfully put my arm around Lanie. "You and I can just go together, right?" I knew it would still technically be like going "without a date," but if we owned it, and told everyone we didn't WANT dates anyway, it would look much better.

Lanie shook her head. "Sorry, sister. I have the distinct feeling that Marc is going to ask me."

I don't know why that thought hadn't occurred to me, based on what Lanie said the other day about Marc acting all flirty with her. But as soon as she said it, my heart dropped. If Bevan was going to ask me, he would have already. I don't think he's planning on going with someone else—because that isn't his style. But I think he just has too much else on his mind to stop

GIVE ME A 73!

We were so wrapped up in our conversation, we didn't notice all the people whizzing past us on their way to class.

"Oops, I gotta go. We're gonna be late," I said.

"Yeah, okay. Well, later then, right?"

"Uh-huh."

I turned around before he could see me smile. I gotta keep him on his toes.

After English class, Lanie and I met in the Lounge. She looks extra adorbs today, wearing a superlong cardigan over shiny stretch pants and knee-high combat boots.

"You like?" she asked, pouting her lips like they do in fashion mags. Unforch, on her the pout just made her look like a fish struggling for water.

"Yeah, I like it a lot. But eighty-six the fish face."

"Ha-ha. So, better start to the week?" asked Lanie. She obviously knew all about Bevan canceling on our bowling date on Friday, and she agreed that it was really rude of him.

"Actually, yes," I said.

"Good. Not to bring you down again, but Bevan's been super lame lately. I'm surprised, though, you know?" she said. "He started out really nice."

"Yeah, I know. But it's not that he's not <u>nice</u>. It's

GIVE ME A 72!

was a real loser move to cancel so last minute."

I was liking this version of Bevan. You know, the really sorry version (even though the sorry version should have come WAY earlier than Tuesday). I stared at him, not saying anything, with my arms across my chest. I figured he could keep talking—especially if I wasn't.

"I want to make it up to you—canceling on you and everything. I made sure I don't have any soccer stuff late tonight. Can you go bowling tonight instead?"

I thought about the many, many exciting activities that I had planned on doing tonight:

1. Dinner with Mom (and who knows? Maybe a surprise guest!)
2. Working on my dress
3. Watching cheer videos

Clearly, it's a no-brainer. It seems bowling won't be the worst way to spend my Tuesday night.

"All right," I said, still keeping my cool. "I'll see if my mom will drive me to the alley after I finish some homework."

Bevan looked relieved.

"Awesome!" he said, flashing his usual faint-inducing smile.

GIVE ME A 7!!

My heart was bursting with happy. Getting such nice compliments from someone like Katie is a huge deal. HUGE!

So of course after our little session, I ran into Bevan AGAIN in the hall. Or rather, he ran into me (literally). I wasn't so excited to see him since his switcheroo of plans yesterday (obvs), but then again, I'm not feeling that bad about yesterday anymore. Maybe it was how cute Evan was last night just wanting to hang out and do work together, or maybe it was what Katie just said to me. Either way, I'm having a much better week so far.

"Oh good," said Bevan, nearly out of breath. "I was hoping I'd find you. I knew you had a free period, and I've been looking all over."

I tried not to get excited over the idea that he'd spent the past hour searching for me. I could just see him looking in the cafeteria, the Lounge, the library, and getting frustrated that he couldn't find me. A tiny part of me was a little happy he had to go through some frustration too.

"What's up?" I asked, willing my face to not look at all happy to see him.

Bevan looked at me with huge, puppy-dog eyes. "Maddy, I was thinking about yesterday, and I realize it

GIVE ME A 70!

We practiced bridges and round-offs until my arms felt like they'd fall off. Too bad we couldn't drag a mat or two into the classroom.

A part of me wonders if Katie enjoys torturing cheerleaders the way an evil villain enjoys watching people suffer.

"You know, Maddy," said Katie, "I'm really psyched about our training together."

"You are?" I asked as I stretched out my back.

"Yeah. You have a lot of potential."

It was really nice to hear her say that. Being around Katie sometimes makes me feel a little insecure about my own cheer skills.

"Thanks, Katie. I really appreciate all your help and everything."

"Well, I'm excited to help you be the best cheerleader you can be. Especially since the Titans will need someone really good if, you know, I leave for dance school."

"You really don't think Clem or Hilary has what it takes?"

Katie sighed. "Don't get me wrong. They're killer cheerleaders. But there's just something missing. An ultimate cheerleader has that special something—maybe it's a personality thing. I just don't think they have it. But you do, Maddy."

GIVE ME A 69!

Tuesday, February 22

Afternoon, in the school hallway

Song Level:

Bowlin' in the Wind

STRIKE!

Day numero dos of training with the Katie Monster. Man, that girl is hard-core to the bone. She makes those trainers on <u>I Used to Be Fat</u> look like sweet grandmas. Between my late nights, Grizzly practice, general stress over the dance, and these training sessions, I might just be a walking zombie.

We met in our secret room, which luckily no one else in school touches, so we found the furniture still pressed against the walls where we'd left it. Hopefully it will stay there, so we don't have to worry about heavy lifting every single time we meet.

"All right," said Katie. "Ready for more?"

I took a deep breath. "Whatever it takes."

"Let's start with making the cleanest, most beautiful round-offs and back handsprings you can muster. We're going to warm up with some bridges."

GIVE ME A 68!

"Hey."

"Hey." I saw my own face on the monitor and realized my long day of workouts had taken a toll on MY hair as well. But since when do I care what Evan thinks of my hair? Apparently since now . . .

"What are you doin'?" asked Evan.

Pause: I didn't want to talk about how I was making a dress for the dance, because that might lead to talking about Bevan, which might lead to what I was SUPPOSED to have done that night. I absolutely did NOT need Evan to know that I'd been rejected like the world's biggest dork. I decided to keep my answer on the vague side.

I held up a piece of the pattern I was working on. "Just a new outfit design. You?"

He held up a notebook with some equations on it. "SuperBoy."

"Yikes."

"Yeah. You, um, want to do work together?"

I felt a blush working its way down my cheeks. Why am I being so weird?? Since when do fashion and comics make me blush?! "Sure," I said.

We eventually got into our own grooves, and just kept each other company for hours while we worked. It was really nice. Maybe even better than bowling.

GIVE ME A 67!

got tons of homework to do."

Tiny lie, but definitely necessary.

Mom actually looked a little bit relieved. Guess she wanted some alone time with everyone's favorite gym teacher (shudder). I **REALLY** hope this doesn't get around school. How embarrassing! I could just see everyone passing stupid notes about this to me in class.

Before I had a mini vomit session, I started to work on my outfit for the Sunshine Dance. I've already decided on a sketch I like, so now it's time to create a pattern to work from. Luckily, I have a pattern I bought a while ago at Sew What (fave store) to base this one on. I'll have to do a little shoppin' over the weekend for fabric. Not that I need an excuse to go to Sew What.

When it was almost time for bed, I hopped on chat to see who was on. I saw Bevan's away message, which of course just reminded me of how he'd canceled on me earlier today. But before I had a chance to get bummed all over again, I got a message from E.

Evan: "Heyyyy! Go on v-chat!"

I went on v-chat, and Evan's face appeared on the monitor. His hair looked like he'd taken a nap on it, even though I'm pretty sure he hadn't. Messy is his hair's natural default. I actually think it suits him.

GIVE ME A 66!

wine. She could definitely tell I was not happy.

"Madington, I didn't realized you'd be home so early. You know, um, Ed."

Ha! His first name is Ed. As in phys ED. It doesn't get any better than that.

"Hello, Miss Hays," said Mr. Datner. He cleared his throat awkwardly. "How was, um, practice?"

I could tell he was as comfortable as I was with our little dinner party.

"It was good," I said, trying to ignore the dorky color-block polo shirt he was wearing. It's not that Mr. Datner is grotesquely ugly or anything (to be honest, I really don't like thinking about his looks at all). He's about Mom's age, and is still steering clear of toupee territory, but the way he dresses makes him look like an old man on a golf course.

"Would you like to join us?" asked Mom.

I noticed Mom had also made sweet potato pie and creamed spinach. She must have really been trying hard to impress Mr. Datner, and I didn't want to ruin things. At least one of us could follow through with her plan tonight! Besides, I'd had a long enough day and really didn't want to stick around for Mr. Datner to order me to do a hundred push-ups.

"Um, I think I'm going to just eat in my room. I've

GIVE ME A 65!

delicious meal for yours truly, since that's pretty much a regular night for her.

When I closed the door behind me, I heard the distinct sound of a man's voice, followed by Mom's laughter.

Unless she was being entertained by some burglar who also happened to be a stand-up comedian on the side, Mom was totally on a date and I was about to witness it!! OMG.

"Mom?" I asked, projecting my voice as much as possible. Maybe the guy would be scared at the possibility of having another witness and would get the heck out of my house.

"In here, honey!"

Since she didn't sound like she was in much danger, I exhaled in relief.

That is, until I saw who was keeping Mom company. "Mr. Datner?" I said. I couldn't help the disgust that was seeping out of my voice. Like, ew with barf on top! I knew that my gym teacher and Mom had some kind of thing going, but the least she could have done was spare me witnessing it. Hello? Nice to tell your daughter that she should expect to see her gym teacher when she gets home.

Mom was smiling ear to ear and holding a glass of

GIVE ME A 64!

Jacqui bit her lip. "Oh. Yeah, of course. Those guys are, like, living, eating, and breathing soccer these days." She paused for a moment before asking, "Are you upset?"

"Yeah, a little. But mainly because we haven't hung out in forever, you know?"

Jacqui waved at her mom in the parking lot. "I wouldn't take it personally, Mads. You know how some people get about sports stuff." She winked and nudged my arm with her elbow.

I do, obviously. I'm one of them. But I can't really help taking it personally.

"Yeah, I guess."

We threw our backpacks in the trunk of her mom's SUV. I was about to open my door, when Jacqui quickly whispered in my ear, "Oh, do me a favor? No guy talk in the car. My mom is super strict about that stuff. She doesn't even like to be reminded that we go to school with boys."

"You got it," I said. And that was totally fine with me. I was done talking about Bevan for the night.

When I got home, I opened the door to the smell of chicken roasting. Mmmmm. I knew Mom had plans tonight, but I didn't think they'd be happening at home. And something told me her "plans" weren't cooking a

didn't have the energy to deal with that sad, sorry look I knew she'd be sporting once she found out that Bevan had canceled on me.

"You want to keep working on it?" I asked Jacqui. Not like I had any plans.

Anymore.

"Sure!" she said.

"Cool. Hey, do you think your mom could give me a ride home after?"

"Of course, no prob."

Jacqui and I put together something simple enough for the whole team but with bits and pieces that looked impressively difficult. It was coming along really well by the time Jacqui looked at the clock and realized her mom would be picking us up any minute.

"You sure you don't mind giving me a ride?" I asked.

"Are you kidding?" said Jacqui. "Your house is on the way. Hey, I thought you had, um, plans tonight?" She wiggled her eyebrows.

"Yeah, well . . ." I forgot I'd told Jacqui why I wouldn't be able to stay late. Ugh. Not that I care if she knows, but I knew that talking about it would just annoy me all over again. I just wanted to get home and not think about the rejection of today. "Bevan had some soccer stuff."

GIVE ME A 62!

which songs were really in the running. It came down to "Teenage Dream" and "Born This Way." Surprisingly, Matt and Ian were much less reluctant to change their votes than expected. After a short whisper session that no one was privy to, both of their hands shot up when "Born This Way" was on the table. Weird. But "Born This Way" won.

"Well, guys, thanks for picking my song," said Jacqui. "I think this will be a fun, upbeat number to create a routine for."

Most of the team hooted excitedly. Except Ian, who grumbled under his breath.

For the rest of practice, Jacqui and I choreographed the first few moments of the routine on the fly.

"Tomorrow I'll bring music so we can put it together with the real beat," said Jacqui, as everyone left for the day.

Mom had to take off a little early, claiming that she had "plans," whatever that means.

"Have fun tonight, sweetheart!" she said to me before she left.

I didn't have the chance to tell her that the Bevan date was off, and I certainly wasn't about to bring it up in the middle of practice. She'll find out eventually, but I

GIVE ME A 6!!

"Well, I think we should do 'Teenage Dream,'" said Diane indignantly.

Ian and Matt groaned in protest.

Jared of course chose "On Any Sunday." Everyone rolled their eyes.

Jacqui put her song in last. "It was a no-brainer for me. 'Born This Way.' I'm a huge Lady Gaga fan." She smiled.

"What about coach?" asked Matt in a half-joking kind of way. "Is she putting in a song request? Hey, Coach C!" he shouted at Mom. "Want to place a vote?"

Mom spoke up from the sidelines. "I don't think you'll appreciate my vote," she shouted back, shaking her head. "Unless you like nineties rock."

"We'll take a pass, thanks," I said. "Guys, seriously. Her favorite bands are Toad the Wet Sprocket and Spin Doctors."

I heard a whole lot of crickets. Everyone looked at me with blank expressions of "wha?"

"Exactly. Coach Carolyn isn't up-to-date on the music scene," I joked.

"Hey, hey," said Mom, walking over. "I was cool in my day. But I get the hint. Keep me out of it."

We went around a second time, but this time no one could vote for their own choice. This way we could see

GIVE ME A GO!

everyone will give their idea for a song. Then we'll go over each one and raise our hands in a vote to pick the winner. Good?"

Everyone nodded yes.

"Madison, you start."

"I say 'Firework' by Katy Perry."

Jacqui smiled. I know she likes that one too.

"Ian?"

Ian looked at Matt. "This is a joint submission, so it has to count twice."

"Okay," said Jacqui.

"'Bottoms Up,'" said Ian.

"Nicki Minaj and Trey Songz, whassup?" Matt said, giving Ian a high five.

"Guys, I don't think Principal Gershon will allow a song about drinking at the school dance," I said. What morons.

"That's our vote," said Ian with a shrug.

Tabitha Sue voted for Justin Bieber's "One Less Lonely Girl."

"Does that feel fast enough to dance to?" Diana asked.

Tabitha Sue put her finger on her lips, thinking. "Sure," she said hesitantly. "We could maybe find a club version that's faster?"

GIVE ME A
59!

cancel on bowling tonight."

"Okayyyy," I said, doing my best not to look disappointed.

"You understand, right?" he said pleadingly. "The guys want to go as late as possible tonight. I can't really say no, you know? But I hate to cancel on you so last minute."

"It's fine, whatever. Look, I gotta get to practice," I replied icily.

Bevan wrinkled his brow. "I'm really sorry," he said again.

Whatever. It isn't the first time he's canceled on me for something soccer related. I know I probably should have been more understanding, since I've had to give up certain social things for cheer. But I always make sure to strike a balance. AND I don't keep canceling on the same person, either. Oh, and one more thing: I ALWAYS make it up to the people I cancel on.

T.G. I had practice to lift my spirits. Today we settled on what song we are going to dance to for the routine. Everyone had their own ideas about what would work best.

Jacqui sat everyone in a circle before we started our usual warm-up.

"Okay, so I'm going to go around the room, and

GIVE ME A 58!

"You got it," I said. "After practice, right?" I'm kind of excited to show off my mad bowling skillz. Is that totally dorky? Oh well.

"Great." Bevan beamed back at me.

I walked away feeling just a little bit better about the whole interaction, but I still have this nagging feeling. . . . Why did it take so long for him to notice me? Is he that hooked on soccer stuff that he is blind to everything else?

In the bathroom, I took a good look in the mirror. Maybe he didn't recognize me—I looked like a DISASTER!

NIGHTTIME, BEDFORDSHIRE

I didn't even have a chance to get too excited about our bowling date tonight because right before practice, Bevan came up to me with a very apologetic look on his face. I immediately knew something was up.

"What's going on?" I asked him. I didn't have a lot of time to chat. Practice would be starting any minute.

"Um," he said, running his hands through his wavy brown hair.

"Yeah?" I said, trying not to laugh. Sometimes I laugh when I'm nervous. I could tell he was nervous too.

"Man, I am so sorry to do this, Maddy, but I have to

GIVE ME A 57!

to say something, but no such luck. Finally, I spoke up.

"Hey, guys," I said.

Bevan looked at me in total surprise. Really?!? "Whoa, Maddy. Where'd you come from?"

"Social studies," I deadpanned. I know I could have been friendlier, but I wasn't feeling like it just then.

"Dude," said his friend Mike. "She's been standing here for, like, an hour."

Um, not so much. But whatever, I think it got the point across.

Bevan flushed, looking clearly embarrassed. "Wow, I must have been on another planet."

I nodded, trying to not show that I was hurt at having been so obviously ignored. I felt like such a loser. An invisible loser.

But then Bevan smiled at me. Not just any smile. Like he was smiling at the best thing in the world kind of smile. If he could radiate light, it would have been giving me a sunburn. That loser feeling left me as I basked in the glow. I'm SUCH a sucker. And right there in front of all his friends he was like, "So I'm gonna see you tonight, right? Bowling for beginners?"

Mike let out a low snicker. "Bowling?"

Bevan gave him a look that would have sent a lion scurrying away.

GIVE ME A 56!

Just then, the bell rang. "I think this was a good start, don't you?"

"Oh yeah. That was great, Katie. Thanks!"

We decided to leave the room separately. I felt like we were spies or something, with all this secretive planning.

Katie left first, and I followed about twenty seconds later. Luckily, the coast was clear. I needed to get to the girls' room stat and fix the rest of my post-workout look. But as I was booking it to the nearest bathroom, who did I see but Mr. Disappearing Act himself: Bevan.

He was standing in a group of his soccer friends. What a surprise! I totally could have snuck past him, but I was worried one of his friends would notice and be like, "Um, why is Maddy pretending not to see you?" I don't care what his friends think, I just don't want them to think it out loud. I decided to be brave and go up to him to say hi. I smoothed my hair and put a smile on my face as I approached the group. He didn't even see me there. One of his friends gave me the "whassup" head nod, but Bevan didn't notice. They were talking about some strategy another school's team had used to win a game, and Bevan was leading the discussion. I stood there looking majorly awkward, waiting for Bevan

GIVE ME A 55!

Katie smiled triumphantly and took a bow. "Then my job is done," she said. "I mean, for now."

"Ha-ha," I said. "So was I really bad at this stuff and I just didn't know it?" My cheer ego was feeling a little deflated.

Katie patted me on the back. "Not at all. But I want you to really knock everyone's socks off at tryouts, so I'm making you work super hard on this stuff. You'll see. There's a method to my madness."

I wiped the beads of sweat from my forehead. "Guess I know where Jacqui learned her drill sergeant style from."

"You got it," she said, with a wink. She went over to her bag and pulled out a pocket mirror, examining her hair. "Ugh, I look like a wet rat," she said, adjusting her nearly perfect braid.

I rolled my eyes. "Puh-leez. You look like you took a light jog down the hallway. I, on the other hand, must look like I ran a marathon."

Katie cocked her head as she looked at me. "Here," she said, handing me her mirror. "Try some powder."

Usually I'm not one to care how I look after practice, but since I'm technically not supposed to be practicing, I had to do some damage control.

"Thanks."

GIVE ME A 54!

flexible person in the whole school. She can touch her ankle to her head, keeping her leg perfectly straight. It looks awesome on the top of a pyramid.

"What are you, Gumby?" I asked her.

Katie giggled. "Oh, I've always been able to do this. I'm naturally flexible. I think that's what made me like dance and gymnastics so much—it came kind of naturally." She shrugged.

Ooh, jealous. The only thing on my body that bends without any pain or training is my floppy ears. "Lucky."

"Okay, so I know you're going to think this is baby stuff, but we're gonna work on the fundamentals. Coach Whipley is insane about proper form and technique. She hates when a cheerleader knows the hardest stunts but can't do a proper toe touch."

"I get it. We're always reviewing that stuff with the Grizzlies, too."

"Well," said Katie, "we're not just going to review it. We're going to perfect it."

We practiced toe touches and pikes for almost an hour. I don't know how I'm going to manage Grizzly practice later. T.G. I have a little time to decompress until then.

"Katie! My legs feel like JELL-O!" I said, massaging my thighs.

GIVE ME A 53!

"Really? I thought her life was, like, perfect."

Katie shook her head, and her eyes widened. "Yeah, right. Once, we had this competition, and Clem was so nervous that her mom would be disappointed in her if she messed up that she stayed up all night practicing, and when it came time to compete, she actually did mess up from being so exhausted. Her mom literally stormed out of the arena and wouldn't talk to her for days."

"Wow," I said. "I had no idea."

"Yeah, I think she just doesn't really get that being nasty to someone isn't okay. She sees how her mom behaves toward her—and since she knows her mom loves her, she thinks that's normal. But she is one of my best friends. Maybe one day you'll see."

"Maybe," I said, but honestly, I'm not so sure. "So, what's on the menu for today?" I said, changing the subject.

Katie smiled. "Well, first we have to move some of this junk," she said, looking at the old desks and filing cabinets that cluttered the room. It looked like this was where school furniture went to die.

We cleared enough space for us to be able to do a couple of more contained stunts. It's not ideal, but it's what we have to work with. Once that was done, Katie and I did our own stretches. Katie must be the most

GIVE ME A 52!

Score!

So Katie and I met up in our "secret" classroom. I was a little worried that someone might see us practicing there, and my secret would be out. I was especially worried that someone might be Hilary. Or worse, Clementine.

"Trust me," said Katie, tying her shoelaces tighter. "When Hilary and Clementine aren't in class, they don't even look at a classroom door. I practically have to text them to remind them to go to their classes."

"Well, I hope you're right," I said warily. "Speaking of Clementine, what's her deal? Why is she so mean all the time?"

Katie looked a little uncomfortable. "She's not always that way."

"Really? Could have fooled me."

"When you get to know her, she can be a really good friend. She's always there for me."

"I don't know," I said. "It seems like she goes out of her way to make people feel terrible, particularly me."

Katie took a seat on one of the desks. "There's something you should know about Clem. She wasn't always like this. But her mom is, like, one of those moms who is always pushing their kids to be the best, and she says the meanest things to her."

GIVE ME A
5!!

spoke up for me, and then looked at me that way, I saw him . . . I don't know. It was just different."

I nodded. I totally knew what she was talking about.

"So maybe he'll ask you to the dance?"

Lanie got this dazed, dreamy look on her face. Then it was like a switch had turned off, and that dreamy look was gone. "Yeah, well, who knows? It doesn't really matter. Whatever."

I could tell she was trying desperately to keep her excitement level at zero. (Maybe she can teach me how to do that?)

I met up with Katie during the free period that we both have. We're supposed to actually go to the library and study during free periods, but we already spoke to Principal Gershon about it. Katie had a brilliant idea to tell Principal G. that we, as captains, were planning a special surprise for our teams, and that we needed privacy to work on it. We told her we were hoping to use one of the classrooms that wasn't being used. If Principal G. actually went to a school game or two, she'd know that this was kind of a bogus idea, but she seemed too distracted with the papers on her desk to question it. "Yes, sure, have fun," she said, waving us out of the office. "Just make sure you make it on time to your next class."

GIVE ME A 50!

'fun' isn't usually my area of expertise, I agreed. I mean, I'd have an interesting perspective, since I'm not like one of those school-dance-obsessed people."

"Um, we'll have to reserve judgment on that until you finish your story," I joked. "Okay, so you're excited about the article, or something else?"

Lanie shook her head in frustration. "No! I mean, yes, I am. But, I don't know, I kind of got the feeling Marc was hinting at something more than just the article. Like maybe he kind of likes me."

I caught Evan glancing at me when Lanie said the word "like."

"You want me to talk to him? Mano a mano?" teased Evan.

"Do and I'll get you back in your sleep!" Lanie hissed.

"Okay, okay," Evan said, backing away with his hands up in surrender. "I was just messing around. Girl it up to your hearts' content, I'm outta here. See you at lunch."

I watched Evan as he walked away, only to see him turn at the last minute and look at me. Lanie was too excited to notice.

We started walking to our classes. "That's great, Lanes, but do you like this guy? I've never heard you mention him before."

The corners of Lanie's lips curled up into a smile. "I didn't like him before, but it was so weird. After he

GIVE ME A 49!

phys ed), but she also doesn't really get excited about things. Usually. Unless the latest issue of <u>Poet's Weekly</u> comes out with her favorite author or something.

Lanie looked at Evan and me to make sure we both had all eyes on her. "Okay," she said. "So I should have known something was up the other day because Marc Derris was acting kind of weird to me. Like, being super nice and everything."

"Slow down. Marc Derris? Who's that?" I asked.

"Oh, sorry," said Lanie. "He's on the <u>Daily Angeles</u> with me."

Evan, who I could tell at this point was getting a tad uncomfortable, since this convo was obviously entering girl-talk territory, actually piped up, "I know Marc. He's in science with me."

Lanie nodded. "Anyway, in our meeting last night, Mr. Samuels was deciding who should write what article, and I wasn't getting any of the assignments. Then the last assignment came up, and it was about the Sunshine Dance. I could tell Mr. Samuels was going to give it to Ricky, because he always writes the 'fun' articles. So I was about to give Mr. Samuels a piece of my mind when Marc was like, 'I think Lanie would do a great job writing that one.' And he was looking at me funny when he said it. Kind of in an intense way. And even though

Friday, February 18

Midmorning, girls' bathroom
(freshening up from secret workout)

Song Level:
(Feelin' the) Blood, Sweat, and Cheers

This morning Lanie came sprinting down the hall while I was at my locker. Lanie doesn't normally sprint (or do anything that might require her heart to pump fast), so I knew something was going on.

"Ohmigod, good, you're here!"

I looked around me. "Yeah, where else would I be?"

Lanie gulped a few breaths of air. "Sorry," she said with a smile. "I meant I was hoping you'd still be by your locker."

"Hey, girls," said Evan, plopping down his bag. He reclined against the locker next to me and took out his sketchbook.

"Oh, good. Evan's here too. So you can both hear my big news!"

We both looked up at her expectantly. Not only does Lanie not do anything remotely athletic (unless she's in

GIVE ME A 47!

As I was flipping through one of my mags, I found the CUTEST sparkly dress in one of the editorials. It was strapless (which is usually not my thing), with a black sequin top and a tiered cream-colored skirt. The skirt had the coolest pattern, and it looked kind of like a tutu. And on top of that it was covered in sequins— but not the cheesy kind. It was SUPER adorable.

I snapped a picture of the dress and sent it to Lanes. In the subject line of the e-mail I wrote, "What do u think?"

"Ohmigod, luvs!"

Yippee!! Okay, so I may not get this boy thing right, but at least I know a thing or two about looking supercute. Next thing I'd have to do was find a pattern. And material! Ack. Lots to do, but I am swearing here and now that I will try my hardest to not get down in the dumps over this Bevan/dance thing. As they say in cheer, P-O-S-I-T-I-V-I-T-Y is the way to be!

GIVE ME A 46!

I shrugged, trying to be all casual. "Not really. Same stuff."

I could see Mom frown a little, out of the corner of my eye. "You've been spending a lot of time in your room lately."

"Oh, yeah. Just working on some sewing stuff."

"Anything I can see yet?"

Ugh. The worst part about lying is when the person you're lying to asks for evidence. And I haven't a "stitch" (ha-ha!).

When I got back home, I decided to distract myself from thinking about my weird night with Evan by leafing through all my fashion mags for inspiration. Which of course got me to thinking about the dance and whether or not Bevan will actually ask me. I can't imagine why he wouldn't. We are still, like, dating and all (we even have an actual date coming up). But if that's the case, then I just don't understand WHAT IS TAKING HIM SO LONG?!? Does he want to be the only one on the soccer team going alone? And why the heck am I worrying about this dress anyway if I'm gonna end up not going to the dance at all? Cuz honestly, the more I think about it, if Bevan doesn't ask me, I'm just gonna stay home. Lanie's right. Sitting next to Abby Lincoln on the bleachers is not a fun way to spend a Friday night.

GIVE ME A
45!

to stick me in headlocks, like, five times a day. But this was different. WAY different. But not in a bad way. Which is so W-E-I-R-D!!!

After dinner, we watched an episode of <u>made</u>, and I could tell that he purposely sat way on the other side of the couch. It was like he was the North Pole and I was the South. It was like the thing that almost happened in his room had never almost happened.

Before I knew it, my mom called, making us both jump (again!) to say she was on her way to get me. On the car ride home, Mom was like, "We haven't talked much lately."

I guess she was right. But I don't really know how I can tell her about my Titan tryouts thing, with her being our coach and all. And since that's the thing mostly on my mind these days, I wasn't really left with much else to say. Okay, fine, yeah, I have the dance on my mind too, but it wasn't like I was gonna get all girl talky with Mom about it.

So instead I just said, "Really? Hmm." And did my best to sing along to the song on the radio so she would think I was just in my own zone.

"Well," she said brightly. "Now that we're finally alone, I figured we could catch up. Anything new?"

Man, she was not giving up easily.

GIVE ME A 44!

cafeteria earlier today with Lanie.

"Yeah, why wouldn't we be?" Evan replied, with a sarcastic tone. "Are <u>you</u>?"

Evan's mom made a face. "Yes, I'm fine, Evan, but there's no need for that tone."

EEK!! Embarrassing! No one likes being lectured by their mom in front of a friend.

"Sorry, Mrs. Andrews. We're kind of dazed from staring at the computer screen for an hour."

Mrs. Andrews worked on cutting her pork cutlet into bite-size pieces. "You kids and your computers. One day your eyes are going to be stuck to those screens and no one will be able to pry them off."

That's a pretty picture ☹.

Evan got up to serve himself a little more. "Evan, save some for your father. He's working late tonight."

"Yeah, yeah," said Evan. "I mean, yes, Mom," he quickly corrected himself. When he sat back down, his knee touched mine by mistake (I think). But get this: He didn't move it. So I didn't move mine away either. I could feel this little tingle where our knees were touching. Not like static, but, like, a good feeling. An insane feeling, considering it was Evan's knee. It's not like Evan and I have never touched before—we used to roughhouse ALL the time when we were kids. He used

GIVE ME A
43!

"Funny. Well, people do love happy endings. I hope SuperBoy gets the girl of his dreams."

"Me too." Evan beamed.

Then this really awkward thing happened where he was smiling at me and I was smiling at him, and neither of us said anything. And then he got this weird look on his face like either he was going to say something, or I don't know, this sounds TOTALLY weird, but it looked like one of those looks you give someone before you're going to kiss them. Can you believe?! I was absolutely terrified. Imagine! Evan and me kissing! But I didn't move or anything, so I guess you could say I was tempting fate. Or, um, Cupid.

Then, like, from another universe, Evan's mom was yelling, "Kiiiiids! Dinner's ready!"

Evan jumped, like, five feet in the air, and cleared his throat. I looked down and arranged the SuperBoy comic in order. "Guess we should go down," I said.

"Yep, guess we should," Evan said, avoiding eye contact.

Oh, sure, NOW he looks away!

Truth? I think we were both relieved to be saved by the (Dinner) Bell.

"You guys okay?" asked Mrs. Andrews, looking from me to Evan. It was oddly similar to the moment at the

GIVE ME A 42!

SuperBoy says to Cupid, "You did that on purpose!" and then Cupid clutches his belly, laughing. I think Evan's Cupid looked a lot like Elmer Fudd, but that's just me.

"It's not finished yet," said Evan, his voice cracking. "But what do you think?"

"Creative!" I said enthusiastically. I like where this one is going. His comics are getting funnier and funnier. "That's one ugly Cupid, though," I added.

Evan laughed. I suggested we try to find a less offensive Cupid, so we spent the next hour surfing the Net for more attractive Cupids. It was hilarious! Not to mention mucho hard. You won't believe how many creepy Cupids there are out there!

Then, in what seemed like an über-delayed reaction, Evan smiled and asked, "But you like it, right?"

"Yeah! I can't wait to see how it ends. Does SuperBoy get revenge on Cupid, or does Cupid get away with it?"

Evan sat down next to me, looking over my shoulder at the pages in my hand. "So, the way I'm seeing this one," he said, "is that Cupid keeps making the wrong people fall in love. Like, the principal falls in love with the janitor, and this popular girl falls in love with the biggest nerd in school. But in the end, Cupid definitely gets what's coming to him."

GIVE ME A 4!!

sat on the edge of his bed. I noted that he still had the same Spider-Man sheets from when he was little. Normally, I'd be all "What a dork!" but for some reason, today it just made me smile.

The cover of this latest SuperBoy installment showed everyone's favorite laid-back hero holding up a thick textbook like a shield, as a Cupid-type figure pointed a bow and arrow at him. The arrow, of course, had a heart on the end of it instead of a sharp dagger. The title of this installment was SuperBoy and the Renegade Cupid.

I looked up at Evan, one eyebrow raised. "A renegade Cupid?" I asked.

Evan cleared his throat. "Just read it."

Okay, here it goes: In the story, SuperBoy has a huge crush on a girl, and he's figuring out the best way to ask her on a date. The comic shows him totally wimping out and running away in one scene, and in another, he gets a really dorky-looking kid to ask her if she likes him. Finally, he figures out he could use a little help from Cupid. So this little Cupid character wearing a mustache and a bow tie flies in. Cupid is supposed to hit the girl with a love arrow to make her like SuperBoy, but he aims at just the wrong second, making her fall in love with a random kid in the hall.

GIVE ME A 40!

Mrs. Andrews nodded like she knew what my mom's "usual" was, even though they'd never really been friends. We caught up on some of my latest cheer stuff, and school stuff, and then she flipped the radio on to a smooth jazz station and started humming along.

"Sorry for the twenty questions," whispered Evan.

"It's cool," I said.

Evan bounded up the stairs to his room as soon as we got home, so I followed.

"Hey, Maddy!" Mrs. Andrews shouted up the stairs. "You stayin' for dinner?"

Evan gave me a hopeful look.

I didn't think Mom would mind. "That sounds great," I said, running down the stairs so I wouldn't have to scream. It's one thing to yell like a banshee in your own house. It's another to do it in someone else's. "Thank you!"

When I got back up to Evan's room, he had flipped on the small light over his desk, illuminating the countless stacks of drawing paper that were strewn this way and that.

"You ready for brilliance?" he asked me, holding a pile of papers to his chest.

"Always," I said.

He extended the papers to me, so I took them and

GIVE ME A
39!

I dropped my bags on the ground next to his. "Hey yourself."

"My, uh, mom should be here any second," he said, scanning the parking lot.

I shrugged. I wasn't in a rush. "No worries," I said.

"I'm psyched to show you the new SuperBoy I've been working on," he said excitedly.

"Oh yeah? So what's this one about?"

He smiled. "You'll see."

"Okay," I said.

Evan's mom honked her horn as she sped into the parking lot. Mrs. Andrews isn't known for her great driving skills. But I never remember her getting into any accidents, and somehow she manages to avoid speeding tickets. Watching her speed into the school lot, I hoped that her lucky streak would at least last until she drove us home.

"Hey, Maddy," she said cheerfully as I heaved my gym bag and backpack into the backseat. "Been a while. How've you been?"

"I'm good!" I told her. Evan rolled his eyes at me, as if to say, "Can't parents just be quiet once in a while?" But I didn't mind.

"How's your mom?"

"She's great," I said. "Just, you know, the usual."

GIVE ME A 38!

Woo-hoo! She's not mad at me AND I get to start training. Win-win.

NIGHTTIME, LIVING IT UP IN MY LIVING ROOM

Just came back from Evan's house. I didn't realize how many hours I'd been there until Mom called, saying it was "last call" for a pickup! Time flies when you're having fun, right? I don't even know what we did the whole time.

Let's rewind: After practice, I went to the locker rooms and actually made an effort to look cute, even though I was sweaty and gross from practice. I know that Evan's seen me at my absolute worst (think not having showered for days when I had the flu last year, in the hospital after I had my tonsils out, etc.), but something made me want to look cute. I used the face blotters Mom gave me a few months ago for the first time (they really work!) and put on some lip gloss.

Evan was waiting in the parking lot, but when he saw me, his face broke out into the biggest grin. He looked adorable, in that rumpled, "no clue" way of his. His button-down checkered shirt was a few sizes too small for him, but it actually showed off the muscles in his arms (which, BTW, I never noticed before).

"Hey, Madison."

I mean, even though we were officially on the same side, since we never compete against each other. Still, there's definitely a subtle rivalry developing between the two teams—especially after Jacqui chose to stay on the Grizzlies even AFTER the Titans apologized for kicking her off and asked her to come back.

"Okay, fine, you have a point," I conceded. "But there's a big difference between giving me a BFF bracelet and aiming darts at my head. Do you think you could just try to be a little more civil?"

"I'm so sorry, you're right. I guess I've just been overcompensating. Clem has been, like, attached to my hip lately. I keep thinking she suspects something, so I guess I've been a little over the top. I'll calm it down, I promise."

Suddenly I was hit with a flash of brilliance. "Hey, I just thought of something," I said, smiling. "We could train together in secret. No one would have to know."

Katie considered this for a moment. "You're serious?" she asked. "You really want to be a Titan that badly?"

"I'm almost positive I'm going to try out. That's about all I know so far. But we don't have much time. If I'm gonna do this, I need to start training now."

Katie nodded emphatically. "All right," she said. "I'm in. I'm not one to break a promise."

GIVE ME A
36!

of leper? You weren't even this nasty when we were in that fight about Bevan."

Katie bit her lip and looked down at the floor. "I'm sorry," she said softly. "I really am." She fidgeted with the bottom of her shirt. "But don't you understand? It's not like I really have a choice."

My expression must have given away the fact that I didn't understand at all. What did she mean, she didn't have a choice?? "I don't understand. Weren't you the one who offered to train me?" I couldn't help it, but I knew my voice had taken on a frustrated tone. "And if I remember correctly, you offered more than a few times."

"Yeah," said Katie. "I know. But then I realized, when we got back, that it just wouldn't be possible."

"What do you mean?"

Katie shook her head in frustration. "Honestly, Maddy, what did you think would happen when people saw us together at school? Have you thought about that at all? I can't get caught training someone from another team. And how do you think the Grizzlies would feel?"

It was true. I hadn't really thought about what the Titans would think, but now that Katie said it, it made sense. They wouldn't want Katie training a Grizzly—it would be like giving an advantage to the opposing team.

GIVE ME A 35!

need to take a vote," he said excitedly. "I already have the song picked out. Picture this." He placed his hands together so that they looked like a frame. "The lights dim, the DJ shuts his music off, we assemble in the middle of the dance floor, and BAM! 'On Any Sunday' from <u>Footloose</u> starts playing over the loudspeakers!"

Everyone looked at Jared like he was speaking an alien language.

"What? Oh, c'mon. You've never seen the musical?" he squeaked.

"Sorry, Jared," I said. "I think we'll have to stick with casting votes."

I lingered around after practice until the Titans were finished too. I absolutely, positively HAD to talk to Katie tonight or I would go out of my mind. I waited until Clementine and Hilary had left for the locker rooms, and it was just Katie putting away the last of the blue mats they used for stunt practice.

Katie didn't see me approaching, so she looked startled when I finally said, "Hey."

"Oh," she said, looking around her as if she was making sure no one saw us talking. When she saw that the coast was clear, her face relaxed. "Hey, Madison."

I took a deep breath. "I just need to know," I said, my voice steady. "Since when did I become some kind

GIVE ME A 34!

something else up our sleeves for Get Up and Cheer!"
She looked around at the squad.

"I agree," I said. "We're not making any decisions
yet. We're just going to learn it." Truthfully, I wasn't
overwhelmed by the idea either. Especially if I was going
dateless as well.

The Testosterone Twins were also unenthused.

"I'll participate and everything during practice," said
Ian. "But there's no way I'm doing a dance routine in
front of the whole school."

"Yeah, me neither," said Matt. "I'd rather show up in
a dress."

"That can be arranged," Jacqui joked.

"You have been known to bring out my softer side,"
Matt quipped back, a goofy smirk on his face.

Ian tossed his friend an odd look. He wasn't the only
one. Jacqui also seemed a bit thrown for a loop. But the
mood was quickly broken.

"You all are such Negative Nancys," grumbled Jared.

"We may be negative," Ian began, "but you're—"

"All right, all right. Enough," Jacqui cut him off
before he could say anything too mean to Jared. "Let's
come back tomorrow with ideas for what song to use,
okay?"

Jared offered his suggestion immediately. "Oh, no

GIVE ME A
33!

is who's going with who. Which is FREAKING ME OUT since I obviously don't have a date yet. Hello? Bevan Ramsey? What's your deal?

Jared proposed that we come up with a choreographed routine to debut at the dance. Like one of those YouTube wedding videos where the guests surprise the bride and groom by doing the entire "Thriller" video.

No one was quite as enthusiastic as Jared about the idea.

"Come on, guys! No one will expect it. It will be hilarious! I even have most of the choreography figured out."

Of course he did.

Diane gave Jared a high five. "I'm in. I think it sounds awesome."

Tabitha Sue shook her head. "I don't. It's embarrassing enough that I'm going by myself to this stupid dance, if I go at all. I don't really feel like making a spectacle of myself."

"Let's think about this a minute, guys," said Jacqui, always the peacemaker. "We've been working on more dance moves than ever in our routines. I think we should at least create the routine. And if we end up deciding to do it at the dance, great. If not, we'll have

GIVE ME A 32!

I shook my head. "I'm still torn. On the one hand, I love the Grizzlies like family. I would feel terrible about letting them down."

"Yeah, but?" said Lanie.

"But on the other hand, I've always wanted to be a Titan. From the beginning, the goal was always to try out again and make the team." The thoughts in my head were forming faster than I could say them. "But I think I chickened out somewhere along the way. I guess I've been terrified about being rejected again. And in true Maddy fashion, I really want to prove that I can do it. You know? Like face my fears and live up to the challenge." The second I said it all out loud, I realized I'm STILL terrified.

Lanie giggled. "Aww, you sound like an after-school special."

"Ha-ha, you're hilarious."

Lanie looked at her watch, signaling it was time to head to class. "Mads, whatever you decide to do, I'll be in the bleachers cheering for you."

"Bring your pom-poms," I said with a wink.

POST PRACTICE, RECOVERING ON THE BLEACHERS

Of course all anyone could talk about at practice was that darn dance. I can't escape it! The main gossip

GIVE ME A 3!!

"Duh! My own creation, of course," I said proudly.

"Of course, but, uh, just in case this is news to you, the dance is just a couple of weeks away. How are you going to make an entire dress between getting ready for tryouts, Grizzly practice, and school stuff?"

"Shhh! Lanie!" I looked left and right to make sure no one heard her. "Keep it down, will ya? I don't need the world to know about tryouts."

"Oh. Sorry."

"Actually, that's what I wanted to talk to you about when I texted you before. I didn't want Evan to hear because he's friends with Katie and all. . . . Things are getting out of control with that girl."

"What do you mean?"

"We basically haven't spoken since we got back from New York. And she's been acting like I'm . . . like I'm . . . Abby Lincoln! She's always giving me the stink eye and avoiding me if I come within ten feet of her."

"Whoa!" said Lanie. "That's harsh. And isn't she supposed to be, like"—she dropped her voice to a whisper—"training you and stuff?"

I nodded my head.

"Double whoa," said Lanie. "That stinks. So, wait. Does this mean you've made up your mind? Are you definitely trying out then?"

GIVE ME A 30!

has only one friend in the entire school, and she's imaginary. I think her name is Penny.

Poor Lanie was on her way to Downersville. I had to jump in before she did something drastic. Like stage a protest against all dances.

"Lanes, let's not talk about dates and stuff like that. What about outfits? Aren't you excited to wear something so totally Lane-tastic that no one else would have the imagination to put together?"

Lanie looked at me from the corner of her eye. "Hmm. Good point. I do like getting dressed up. . . ."

Evan rose from the table, his tray in hand. "All right. Girl-talk time. See you later!"

We waved good-bye to Evan.

Lanie turned to face me. "Let's say I do go to this horrible dance. What do you think would work better? Tuxedo pants and a vintage 1940s-style top? Or should I go more traditional with a velvet pantsuit? Fitted, of course."

I did my best to picture the two choices in my head. Only Lanie.

"I'd go with the tuxedo pants and top if I had to choose," I said. "But have you considered a dress?"

"Okay, Fashion Police, what are you thinking of wearing?" asked Lanie.

GIVE ME A 29!

still be nice to not always have to go to them alone," Lanie agreed.

"Lanes, the last dance we went to was our recital for ballroom dance class, when we were, like, seven. And I think I was your date."

Evan laughed, which made a piece of his rigatoni fly out of his mouth onto the table. "Now that is something I would have paid to see."

Lanie rolled her eyes. "Trust me, only Maddy was good at it. I looked like a total spazz."

I slapped Lanie on the shoulder. "Nah, you were great!"

"Yeah, yeah. Anyway, I'm thinking I'm not gonna go to this thing after all."

She tried to say it like it was so not a big deal, but I know Lanie.

"Lanes!" Evan and I said at the same time. "C'mon."

Lanie crossed her arms over her chest. "I can see it now. I'll be sitting on the bleachers next to Abby Lincoln while everyone else slow-dances to Florence and the Machine."

Side note: Abby Lincoln is the gawkiest girl in our class. She's notorious for wearing these awful sweaters with kittens on them, every day WITHOUT fail. Like the kind your aunt would buy you for your birthday that you would never be caught dead in. She

GIVE ME A 28!

Lanie turned to me, with a concerned expression on her face. "Oh yeah? Dish."

But I didn't want Evan to hear me whine about Katie. Foot in mouth much? "Oh, just some dumb quiz I was so not prepared for at all in Hobart's class."

"Really?" asked Evan. "I didn't have a quiz in mine."

"Um, uh," I stammered. "It was a special quiz. Just for our class. Because most people didn't do their homework." I tried to smile but knew it looked insincere.

It was a good thing Lanie wasn't done with her I-Hate-the-Sunshine-Dance speech.

"I just feel like the whole school has a one-track mind these days. I can't even go to the bathroom without hearing about someone's stupid dress or date."

Again, at the word "date," Evan stole another glance at me. T.G. Lanie didn't notice these awkward eye contact exchanges!

"Yeah, it is a little out of control," I agreed.

"Luckily, guys don't have to worry about dresses and stuff like that," said Evan.

"You are lucky," said Lanie. "It's totally different for guys."

"And you can go alone and no one will think you're a loser, because guys are the ones who ask the girls," I added.

"True. And even though dances are lame, it would

GIVE ME A 27!

"Um, yeah! That would be cool."

Inside my head I did a little "V is for Victory" dance. Something good finally happened today!

We made our way to our usual table, and lo and behold, there was Lanes.

Lanie looked from Evan to me, and then back to Evan. "Whoa, did I just miss something? Why are you both blushing? Did you both, like, trip over milk on the way over here?"

Ack! Awkward. Must change subject fast.

"Excuse me, missy, but is there a reason you didn't answer my text before?"

Lanie held up her phone and rolled her eyes. "I would have, if my phone hadn't just coughed its last breath."

Oops.

I sat down and mixed my marinara sauce around my plate until the whole thing was a pinkish-rose color. It was a pasta masterpiece!

"So," said Lanie. "Is anyone else here going to barf if one more person mentions the stupid Sunshine Dance?"

As soon as the words escaped her mouth, I caught Evan looking at me, but when he saw me notice, he coughed and looked away.

"I've kind of had other problems to deal with today," I said.

GIVE ME A
26!

counter. "Well, me, I love taking a baked potato with all the fixins' and melting everything together in the microwave." He winked. "It's my special secret."

I patted him on the back. "Be careful, buddy," I whispered. "People on line might hear you."

"Good call. You always have my back," he said, smiling at me. "Literally."

And not to say that Evan doesn't smile when we're together, but this smile looked a little different from his usual. He seemed downright giddy.

"Duh, what are friends for?" I said.

"Speaking of . . . friend, we haven't hung out in a while."

I could sense Evan getting a little nervous. Like he was afraid I might say I was busy with Bevan. Which has definitely happened in the past, so I guess I understand.

"I know! What's up with that?" I asked innocently.

Evan shrugged. "Anyway, you want to, like, um—" He took a breath. "You wanna hang out sometime this week? Maybe tonight, after practice and stuff?"

Obviously Evan and I had hung out once or twice (or try hundreds) of times. But THIS time, the way he asked felt different. I felt different. Literally, my heart was booming out of my chest at the idea of hanging out just the two of us. Bizarro.

GIVE ME A 25!

as she could at lunch, she was **NOT THERE!** Some friend **SHE** is (I joke, I joke). I hope she has a good excuse for leaving me hangin'. Like, maybe she fell into her locker by mistake and got trapped inside?

Or maybe a pack of wild emo kids kidnapped her and gave her those huge, obnoxious bangs they all wear, and she couldn't see her way to the cafeteria?

Whatever. I'm annoyed that she's not here for her BFF in my time of need.

Feeling alone and friendless (okay, I'm being dramatic), I made my way to the lunch line. It was a good day in terms of lunch choices: pasta bar or build-your-own baked potato. I didn't think either of those choices allowed for the mean cafeteria ladies to throw slime, monkey guts, or mystery meat into the recipes (unlike when they serve Bratwurst Surprise). Yum!

I was waiting in line for my fettuccine Alfredo with a splash of tomato sauce (delish!) when Evan popped up behind me in line. I'm pretty much always happy to see Evan, but today I was hoping to get to Lanie before he showed.

"So," he asked. "What'll it be?" He pointed to the different lunch options. "Door number one or door number two?"

"Oh, I'm all about the pasta bar. Baked potato? Eh."

He grabbed a lunch tray from the edge of the

GIVE ME A 24!

a little switch go on. A switch that says "Act Mean to Maddy Now!"

That's when I realized that maybe Katie doesn't want to treat me this way. Maybe it's all just an act. But still, I don't know the reason behind it.

Katie read the letter as Clementine watched her. Katie folded it back up, shrugged, and made the "crazy in the head" motion with her finger and shoved it into her pocket. Obvs she was calling me loco.

It's beyond ridiculous!

After class I put my books in my bag and waited for Katie to walk past me. I was going to grab her and tell her we need to talk, but she flew out of class like someone had planted a stink bomb. Or, actually, like the stink bomb was me.

Katie wasn't going to let me talk to her. At all. I am fuming! She has a lot of nerve! I need to catch Lanes before lunch and tell her what's going on—I don't want to do it when Evan's around. Not because I like keeping secrets from him, but I know he's friends with Katie so . . . more later!

AFTER LUNCH, IN THE CAF

Even though I texted Lanes that this was an emergenceeee, and that she should meet me as early

GIVE ME A 23!

episode in New York. But I thought Katie and I had an understanding about Titan tryouts. We shared stuff with each other. Secrets. I know she hasn't told anyone on her team about her trying out for dance school. Does she think maybe I told someone and this is her way of getting back at me? Why did she even offer to train me in the first place, and say all that nice stuff about what a good cheerleader I am, if she planned on acting this way once we got back to school? It doesn't make an ounce of sense.

Anyway, I decided to try to find out what her big problemo was. When Mr. Hobart was busy writing out an extremely long and complicated equation (his favorite kind) on the blackboard, I took my chance. I quickly wrote a little note to Katie and ripped it out of my binder.

I passed it to the person behind me and motioned for that person to pass it to Katie. Katie saw me point to her, and she actually didn't make a face. It looked like she was impatient to get the note. Weird! I watched the note make its way toward the back of the classroom, when of course, Clementine grabbed it. Katie looked scared for a minute. But as soon as Clementine turned to hand it to her, Katie's expression quickly went from fear to disgust. It was like I was watching

GIVE ME A 22!

day, it becomes your designated spot (unofficially), so you better like it. I don't make up the rules; it's just the way it is here in Port Angeles. Katie and Clem, who are also in my class (lucky me!), have always sat diagonal from me. But lately, they've both moved to the extra chairs in the last row of the classroom. (Apparently, rules don't apply to them.) I have a feeling it has something to do with me, because whenever Clem and Katie walk by, they snicker as they pass me, and practically sprint to their new seats. It's like I'm the kid who peed in her pants who everyone else wants to avoid.

Right after I sat down, Katie and Clem walked into class. Of course, **THEY** didn't seem to be in any kind of rush. Mr. Hobart has a soft spot for the Titans, so they sauntered in, taking their time. Clementine actually stopped by the window to gaze at her reflection and fluff her hair. Ugh.

So then, they both purposely walked past MY desk, which is totally unnecessary. As Clementine passed me, she mumbled "Ew," and Katie laughed.

I can't stand it anymore. **WHY, OH WHY, AM I THEIR NEW FAVORITE PUNCHING BAG?**

It's not like I expected us to be trading friendship bracelets after we got back from our little bonding

GIVE ME A 2!!

a step in the dance direction," she added.

She must have seen me looking all distant because she quickly said, "Remember, he's a dude. Dudes don't live for things like dances. Not like girls do." She lowered her eyes. "I mean, girls except for me."

"Okay, Miss I-Think-I-Want-to-Go," I snarked.

Just then we saw everyone scurrying to class. "Guess we should mosey on to Torture Session Number One," I said.

Lanie patted me on the back. "He'll ask you, don't worry."

"Yeah, yeah . . . we'll see."

I was almost the last person to arrive at Mr. Hobart's class, and everyone knows that Mr. H is a total dragon about people being late. I once heard about this one kid who was always late. Mr. H made him solve every problem in a math book before he was allowed to leave detention. He actually made the kid come back the next afternoon to finish up! I'm actually surprised Mr. H didn't just make him spend the night. Imagine, having to spend a night with Mr. Hobart. Talk about a nightmare sleepover!

I took my usual seat three rows from the front of the classroom. It's been my seat this whole year. The rule is, once you choose your seat on the first

GIVE ME A
20!

The excitement must be infectious or something, because brace yourself—I think I want to go."

"I can just see it now, you entering the dance in a sparkly hot-pink dress and breaking it down to a techno beat."

Lanie laughed. "Right. That's exactly what'll happen. So . . ." she looked at me expectantly. "I assume you'll be going with B?"

Funny . . . with all my excitement about the dress-up part of the dance, I hadn't even thought about the whole date part.

"Well, actually . . . not as of yet," I said, shaking my head with a frown. It seems I'm not the only one who's on Sunshine Dance delay. Hmph.

Lanie made a face like it was no biggie. "Well, you know Bevan. He's probably just been so into his sports that the dance hasn't made it to his brain yet."

I chewed the inside of my lip, trying to think back to our conversation last night. Why hadn't he just asked me then? Maybe he wanted to wait for our bowling date to ask me in person. . . .

"The good news is, he <u>finally</u> asked me to go out on another date. I was starting to think he'd forgotten my screen name."

"Ooh, that's good," said Lanie, perking up. "Definitely

GIVE ME A
19!

by surprise? Oh. Yeah. Right. Maybe it has something to do with my secret training for Titan tryouts. Guess I've been a little preoccupied (u think?) If there's one thing I like more than anything (or at least as much as cheer), it is dreaming up an outfit for a fun occasion. And this is the occasion of occasions!

I started to mentally flip through the pages of dresses that I've been dying to design but haven't had a reason to wear. (I've got quite a catalog up there.)

Suddenly, a voice interrupted me. "So did you see the posters are finally up?"

I turned to see Lanie, fighting hard to not be at all excited about the dance of the year. Dances and ordinary social events are not Lanie's thing. HOWEVER, I know that deep down, Lanie Marks is just as excited as, say, Clementine Prescott is at the idea of getting glammed up (in Lanie's own way, of course) and maybe dancing with a boy. She is human, after all (or at least I think so).

"Yeah," I said, fiddling with my locker combination to jumble up the code. "Did you know this was coming so soon? Because those posters are the first I've heard of it."

Lanie rolled her eyes. "Have you been living under a pom-pom? It's all anyone ever talks about these days.

GIVE ME AN 18!

poster for the annual Sunshine Dance that's just three weeks away.

Here's the thing: The Sunshine Dance is a HUGE STINKING DEAL. This isn't a girls-on-one-side-of-the-dance-floor-boys-on-the-other kind of dance. It's the first serious dance anyone ever goes to at our school. This will be my first time going to it. Everyone knows that people will be dressed in their absolute best outfits, and EVERYONE who plans on going will be going with a date.

As I stood there pondering my dilemma, two girls came skittering to a screeching halt in front of the poster.

"Ohmigod!" one girl squealed. "Only a couple more weeks! And I don't even have shoes yet!"

Um. Shoes? I didn't even remember it was HAPPENING until two seconds ago.

"Seriously," her friend said. "You better get shopping before they're all out of cute stuff. I bought my dress and shoes months ago. And my dad reserved us a limo. Eeeeeee!"

Dress? Shoes? LIMO? I am so behind.

I walked in a daze toward my locker, wondering how I missed this. I'm sure people have been talking about this dance for weeks now, and I've just been oblivious. Really, how does something like this take me

GIVE ME A 17!

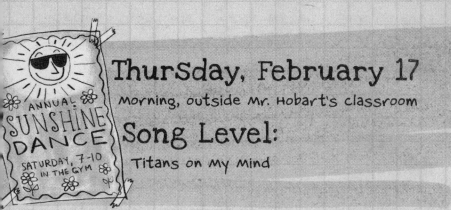

Thursday, February 17

Morning, outside Mr. Hobart's classroom

Song Level:
Titans on My Mind

This morning I was still in a pretty good mood from my convo with Evan last night, PLUS the fact that Bevan actually acknowledged that I exist and asked me out for tomorrow. Things were going well for little ol' moi, Madison Hays. I ate a delish breakfast (Pop-Tarts all the way), tried to ignore the goofy way Mom was acting all morning (parents are weird), AND when we got in the car, my fave song was on the radio (I heart Bruno Mars). Not a bad start to the day, right?

Sigh. Little did I know that surprises awaited me at the school of Doom. I sashayed through the big clonking doors at school and found myself face-to-face with a poster. It wasn't just an ordinary poster—nothing like those neon-colored flyers that people throw all over the school's walls advertising "Math Club Party!" or "Save the Lizards of Laos!" Nope. I was face-to-face with a

GIVE ME A 16!

there. My mind had wandered to Evan. Before I had a
chance to IM him, a message popped up on my screen.
Here's our convo:

    Evan: "Hey u!"

My heart actually skipped a beat. What is happening
to me?

    Maddy: "Hi!"

    Evan: "Whatchu up 2?"

    Maddy: "Meh. Not much. Just hangin'. Soooo tired."

    Evan: "Grueling Grizzly practice?"

Ugh. I hate lying, but I'm not ready to tell him about
my plan to possibly try out for the Titans.

    Maddy: "Yuppers."

    Evan: "☹."

    Maddy: "Totes."

    Evan: "U should relax. I'll check on u l8r."

He is sooo sweet, thinking about me like that.

    We said good-bye and signed off. Finally! Time to
really pass out. I closed my computer and went to take
off my earrings. When I looked in the mirror, I saw
that I was smiling ear to ear.

    And you know what? This smile isn't from Bevan
asking me out to go bowling. It's from talking to Evan!!!
Gah! Cray-zee-ness.

GIVE ME A
15!

I might be wrong, or imagining things (wouldn't be a first!), but I think he actually sounded a little hurt. Like he wanted me to notice and care that we hadn't chilled in a while. I don't know why I didn't just tell him that I was kinda upset that he's been so busy. Maybe I didn't feel like letting him see that he hurt my feelings.

"Yeah," I said. "I guess. You're right, it's been a while. It sounds like you've been really busy."

Awkward pause.

"So. Yeah," he continued. "I was wondering if you wanted to, um, go bowling Friday night?"

Bowling? How cute! Bevan had told me he's only been bowling, like, once in his life. So I guess he's not afraid to look stupid in front of me. I'd told him I'd show him a thing or two.

"Yeah, I think I'm free," I said (playing hard to get, ha-ha). "Let's do it."

"Cool."

"Cool."

"So, I'll see you at school tomorrow?" he asked.

"Yep. I don't plan on being a delinquent."

I was glad he called, but then, for some reason, I decided to go online and see who was there. And now I realize, I wasn't just looking to see if "just anyone" was

GIVE ME A
14!

Lo and behold, it was from Bevan. He left me a voicemail and everything! I was half expecting an automated message, like (cue robot voice that mispronounces everything), "Hello. Madisone. This is an automatic message from Bev and Ramsey. I am sorry that I have not called you in many days. Soccer has taken. Over my life." But luckily, it wasn't automatic. It was **THE BEVAN RAMSEY** in the flesh (or in the voice, I should say) asking me to call him when I got a chance.

I called him back, and he picked up. I'm so awkward at leaving messages, so I was really glad.

"Whadup, Madison?" he said. "You got my message?"

"Yeah, I did. What's goin' on?" I asked, trying to be über-casual. Which was the opposite of what I was feeling inside. In my head I was like, "Where have you been for the past few weeks? Why have I become yesterday's news?"

"Listen, I'm uh . . . sorry I've been such a stranger lately," he said awkwardly.

"What do you mean?" I asked, totally lying. Duh! Like I haven't noticed.

"Well, you know. We haven't been hanging out much lately. My team is really bringing things to the next level. Wait, so, you haven't, like, noticed?"

GIVE ME A 13!

been mucho busy with soccer stuff. I don't think that team even leaves the gym. Maybe they set up sleeping bags and work out until they all fall asleep on the gym floor?

I totally get being obsessed with a sport (I mean, hello!) but still, it's annoying that his obsession is affecting ME! I don't like being the thing that gets thrown to the curb. I think what really sucks is that I'm kind of not sure if I feel the same way I did about him before, and the less I see him, the more true that realization becomes. It's totally not his fault that I had a BIG EUREKA moment about my feelings for Evan while I was away. But it would help if we actually spent some time together—because then I could actually figure out if I feel more for Evan than I do for Bevan, or vice versa.

All right, my brain is now officially closed for the night. I can't take anymore today! Can't wait to get home and just CRASH!

NIGHT, CHILLAXING IN MY ROOM

Are you there, cheer gods? It's Madison! Oh wait. You're actually LISTENING?! Guess so, because right after I inhaled a delish meatball sub and lay down comatose on my bed, I saw I had a MISSED CALL!

GIVE ME A 12!

also laid the Evan thing to rest too (wow, do I sense a pattern here?). So that isn't it. List time!

* Did I toilet paper her house? No.
* Did I come to school dressed in the same outfit as her? Hardly.
* Did I spill orange juice on her pants at lunchtime so that it might look like she had a different kind of accident? Negative.

Speaking of Bevan, I don't really want to admit it to myself, but I don't have a choice anymore: This thing with Bevan is bothering me way more than I thought it would. Maybe it's the exhaustion speaking, but I'm a teeny weenie bit upset that he's been so MIA since I got back. I don't really get it—before I went away, we were like **THIS CLOSE**.

But since I got back we have barely made any plans, and I basically see Mr. Hobart more than I see him. (Which is totally unfortunate, because Bevan is way cuter than Mr. Hobart.)

I couldn't help but look for him in the hall when I left the gym. He used to practically always meet me after practice, which I loved because it was never a planned thing. He'd just be there. Lately, I guess he's

GIVE ME AN
!!!

using both feet to take off from. I'm pretty sure we started to learn this before Diane got here, but no one was near mastering it.

"Okay, so first I'm gonna show you how it looks, and then I'll break it down."

We all cleared some space to give Diane room. Diane took a breath and, without any momentum, flipped in the air, landing perfectly. Not a wobble in sight. Nice!

Jared started clapping, and the rest of the team followed suit.

"Thanks, Diane!" said Jacqui. "Maybe we can all work on this one, huh, guys?"

Everyone looked game, though Jared and Tabitha Sue both had slightly freaked-out looks on their faces. I love it when the team is pumped about learning new things. We divided up into groups again to practice the move. Out of the corner of my eye I saw Katie and Hilary walking into the gym. I learned my lesson from before, not to smile or wave or anything (unless I have a big desire to feel like a loser). So I pretended not to notice Katie. But then she turned her head and saw me and she actually **ROLLED HER EYES** at me! Can you believe?? What did I do to her? I'm racking my brain to figure it out. I know we smoothed things over a superloooooong time ago about the Bevan thing, and that

GIVE ME A
10!

Jacqui smiled. "Oh, totally. I hope everything's okay with you guys."

When it comes to guy stuff, you don't have to say much. Your girls just automatically understand.

I nodded my head, hoping she'd change the subject.

"But listen, Mads, you have to keep it together during practice. Jared could have gotten hurt."

"Yeah, I know. It was my bad. I'm really sorry."

I forced myself to bring my A-game to the rest of practice. But I think after what happened with Jared, the rest of the team wasn't super eager to do anything aerial without Jacqui around. I don't exactly blame them.

Diane somewhat saved the day when she asked if she could show us a new move she learned from a cheerleader friend back in her old town. I'm happy that she decided to stay on the team even after Katarina passed her social studies test and we didn't end up needing a backup member after all. It's cool having another person with a solid gymnastics background on the squad.

"All right, guys, you've probably heard of the punch front," said Diane. "But since we haven't done it yet, I thought I'd show you."

Side note: A punch front is basically a front flip,

Jared bounced on his butt and landed with his legs splayed out on the floor.

"Ow!" he squeaked. "Someone help me up."

I rushed over to his side and told him not to move. Jacqui came running over too.

"You okay?" she asked, her forehead crinkling with worry.

Jared sighed dramatically. "I think I bruised my ego."

Jacqui laughed. "All right, easy getting up. Go get some water."

I patted Jared on the back. "Sorry, dude. That was totally my fault. I should have been spotting you."

"No worries," he said, as he limped away.

I knew Jacqui would have something to say about this. I was right.

"Mads, what happened?" she asked. "You don't seem yourself today."

I shook my head. "No, I'm not. I'm really sorry. I was up tossing and turning all night. I slept for, like, two hours."

"Something wrong?" she asked, searching my eyes for an answer.

I laughed. "Nah." I shrugged. "Not really. Just, you know, Bevan stuff." It wasn't a total lie. I had been thinking about me and Bevan a lot lately, but more on that later.

GIVE ME AN 8!

had an energy drink, and I feel like I can't do anything fast enough."

Tabitha Sue tightened a shoelace and shook her head. "Well, enjoy it while it lasts. Those things can make you crash. Hard."

Tabitha Sue was sooooooo right. By the time I moseyed into the gym, I could feel my energy draining out of me like a leaky faucet. I was dragging my feet by the time I reached the rest of the team.

I did my best to be perky for warm-up, but by the time we got to practicing round-offs with the team, I was yawning like it was my job. I know this isn't, like, the biggest deal in the world. People have tired days all the time. It's just that I ALWAYS have energy for cheer. So when I have an off day, it's really obvious.

Jacqui and I divided the teams into groups of two to practice round-offs. We've been working on them forever, but still, some peeps have been a little sloppy on the finish. I was in charge of Jared and Ian. Jared began his running start and then went into a hurdle before turning upside down. I totally should have seen it coming—his arms weren't high enough in the hurdle, and he was going too slowly into the round-off. I also should have been spotting him, but since my brain was mush, I was standing off to the side. Bad captain!

GIVE ME A 7!

last class of the day I could feel myself slipping into dreamland again, so I spent most of class pinching my arm and poking my hand with the tip of my pencil (works like a charm, BTW). I couldn't imagine how I'd make it through practice. I went over to the vending machine and bought one of those crazy energy drinks that claim to turn you into Road Runner (meep meep!) for five hours. "Yeah," I said to myself. "That's exactly what I need to get through practice."

It worked for, like, five minutes. For five whole minutes (basically, the time it took me to get ready for Grizzly practice), I felt a blast of energy course through my veins. I tore open my locker while untying my hot pink Cons, and at the same time started doing a leg stretch.

"Hey, Maddy, you okay?" asked Tabitha Sue. She was looking at me funny (I'm sensing a pattern here . . . more on that later).

"Yeah!" I exclaimed. I practically ripped off the cute Empire waist top I was wearing and started to put on my shorts. "Never been better!"

Tabitha Sue pointed at my legs. "You sure?"

I looked down. Oops. Forgot to take my pants off. That would help, huh?

I blushed, embarrassed. "Thanks, Tabitha Sue. I just

GIVE ME A 6!

for the Titans is all on me. Well, obviously, whether I make the team or not is my problem, but it would have been nice if Katie decided to live up to her promise of training me. In the meantime, I've been secretly studying up on the Titans: rereading their <u>Spirit Rules</u> book, watching videos of Titan practices and competitions, and dropping by some of their practices. Last night I watched their Regionals routine for about the thousandth time. If I'm going to have a chance of kicking butt at tryouts, I know I'll have to be able to do everything on that video. That is, if I do end up trying out. I haven't even told anyone I'm thinking about it yet. And I CANNOT tell the Grizzlies, like, ever. I feel terrible keeping this big secret from my team. This secret makes me feel, like, the opposite of being a team player. It is sooooo hard going to Grizzly practices knowing that my mind is slightly focused on another team. Talk about NOT being a team player, how about being a traitor co-captain! Wonder what Mr. Cooper would have had to say about my problem had I actually answered his question earlier today?

LATER THAT DAY, SNARKING IN THE PARKING LOT

Um. Yeah. So let's just say I wasn't at my best today during practice. I feel like dog poop. By my

GIVE ME A 5!

trip, when Katie Parker (capitán of los Titans!) planted the idea in my head that I'm some kind of super-awesome cheerleader—Titan material even—I've been thinking about trying out for the Titans. Like, a lot.

Here's the major unfortunate thing: Katie had been all, "I'll train you when we get back home!" when we were in New York, but now that we're back, she's been treating me like I have the bubonic plague (see? I pay attention in class).

Just the other day I passed her sitting with Clementine Prescott (Titan Triumvirate #2) and Hilary Cho (Titan Triumvirate #3) on the way to my table in the caf, and even though she hasn't been so nice since we got back from New York, I couldn't help but give her a smile as I walked by. The entire table was SILENT as I made my way past them. The kind of silent that makes you feel like maybe they've been talking about you (and PS—it wasn't about how great your outfit looked that day). And as soon as I passed them, they all burst out laughing. Luckily, I didn't have to slink away like a giant loser to sit by myself. My BFFs Lanie and Evan were already at our table, so I hightailed it to them, trying to hide my beet-red face behind my lunch tray.

So anyway, Katie's 'tude means that my tryout

GIVE ME A 4!

nostrils flaring, and saying, "Madison Hays, would you like to explain specifically what the rest of us 'don't understand'?"

Oh no. I said that OUT LOUD?

I wiped the drool from the side of my mouth and heard some snickers echo around me. The ENTIRE CLASS was staring at me!!!

"Um, sorry, Mr. Cooper," I said, hoping the redness in my face wasn't too obvious.

He gave me an angry "hmph" and walked back to the front of the classroom. T.G.

Then Sylvie Harris was like, "Nice dream, Sleeping Beauty?"

Ugh. Wanted 2 die.

I should have known better than to have stayed up practically all night last night. No, I wasn't watching She's the Man for the millionth time or catching up on my Teen Vogues. Instead I was glued to YouTube, watching a gazillion cheer videos. Titan spring tryouts will be here before I know it. In a month, to be exact, and I need to be on point this time—I mean, if I do decide to audition.

It's not like I'm 100% ready to go to the Dark Side. I'm still torn about trying out at all, and what I would do if I even made the team. But ever since my New York

GIVE ME A 3!

He looked around the classroom expectantly. Luckily, he didn't look at me.

Jeremiah Ramirez waved his hand in the air frantically. Typical. He looked like he was straining to give his answer. Like if he wasn't picked, he might actually pass out.

"Has anyone besides Jeremiah done their homework?" Mr. Cooper asked wearily. He let out a big sigh. "Okay, Jeremiah, yes?"

And just as Jeremiah was giving his answer, I must have passed out, because suddenly I wasn't in class anymore. I wasn't even ME anymore. I was Boo Radley (yikes! A dude!), sitting in a courtroom dressed in a Titans uniform.

Tabitha Sue Stevens (one of my Grizzly teammates) was the prosecutor, and she was pointing at me and yelling something. Then I realized that the whole jury was made up of the Grizzlies, who were shouting at me.

"Traitor!" the crowd yelled. "How dare you switch teams!"

"But you don't understand!" I said (not as myself but as Boo Radley, of course). "I can explain!"

And here is the mega embarrassing part: I must have been talking in my sleep, because when I opened my eyes, Mr. Cooper was standing right over me, hairy

GIVE ME A 2!

Wednesday, February 16

~~Spirit~~ Song Level:

Sweet Dreams Are Made of Cheer (usually)

OMG, I just had an MEM (mega embarrassing moment). There I was, innocently sitting at my desk in Mr. Cooper's class. I had my notes open on my desk (because I'm studious! Ha-ha) and my eyes were totally focused on what Mr. Cooper was writing on the board. I mean, I even noticed when he tried to pick a booger out of his nose but pretended he was just scratching an itch.

Well, the thing is, I was **TRYING** to be totally focused on Mr. Cooper. But there was a tiny problemo: I was totally exhausted! My eyes kept doing that droopy thing (hot!) and my body would start to sway, and then I'd pinch myself to get alert again.

"Can someone describe some of the ways in which Boo Radley's character represents the theme of innocence in To Kill a Mockingbird?" asked Mr. Cooper.

GIVE ME A !!